Dear Reader,

As one of the wealthiest and most powerful
men in Texas, I not only know exactly what I
want out of life, I usually get it, too. Now, for
the first time in my life, I'm stymied. The
woman I want more than any other won't give
me the time of day.

Michaelann Frazer's no lady—she's sassy,
smart-mouthed and willful. She doesn't fit the
mold of the women I usually date, but then,
I've never met anyone quite like her. She's a
challenge all right, and that excites me.

Sincerely,

Devlin Wingate, President
Wingate Industries, Inc.

1. ALABAMA
Full House • Jackie Weger
2. ALASKA
Borrowed Dreams • Debbie Macomber
3. ARIZONA
Call It Destiny • Jayne Ann Krentz
4. ARKANSAS
Another Kind of Love • Mary Lynn Baxter
5. CALIFORNIA
Deceptions • Annette Broadrick
6. COLORADO
Stormwalker • Dallas Schulze
7. CONNECTICUT
Straight from the Heart • Barbara Delinsky
8. DELAWARE
Author's Choice • Elizabeth August
9. FLORIDA
Dream Come True • Ann Major
10. GEORGIA
Way of the Willow • Linda Shaw
11. HAWAII
Tangled Lies • Anne Stuart
12. IDAHO
Rogue's Valley • Kathleen Creighton
13. ILLINOIS
Love by Proxy • Diana Palmer
14. INDIANA
Possibles • Lass Small
15. IOWA
Kiss Yesterday Goodbye • Leigh Michaels
16. KANSAS
A Time To Keep • Curtiss Ann Matlock
17. KENTUCKY
One Pale, Fawn Glove • Linda Shaw
18. LOUISIANA
Bayou Midnight • Emilie Richards
19. MAINE
Rocky Road • Anne Stuart
20. MARYLAND
The Love Thing • Dixie Browning
21. MASSACHUSETTS
Pros and Cons • Bethany Campbell
22. MICHIGAN
To Tame a Wolf • Anne McAllister
23. MINNESOTA
Winter Lady • Janet Joyce
24. MISSISSIPPI
After the Storm • Rebecca Flanders
25. MISSOURI
Choices • Annette Broadrick

26. MONTANA
Part of the Bargain • Linda Lael Miller
27. NEBRASKA
Secrets of Tyrone • Regan Forest
28. NEVADA
Nobody's Baby • Barbara Bretton
29. NEW HAMPSHIRE
Natural Attraction • Marisa Carroll
30. NEW JERSEY
Moments Harsh, Moments Gentle • Joan Hohl
31. NEW MEXICO
Within Reach • Marilyn Pappano
32. NEW YORK
In Good Faith • Judith McWilliams
33. NORTH CAROLINA
The Security Man • Dixie Browning
34. NORTH DAKOTA
A Class Act • Kathleen Eagle
35. OHIO
Too Near the Fire • Lindsay McKenna
36. OKLAHOMA
A Time and a Season • Curtiss Ann Matlock
37. OREGON
Uneasy Alliance • Jayne Ann Krentz
38. PENNSYLVANIA
The Wrong Man • Ann Major
39. RHODE ISLAND
The Bargain • Patricia Coughlin
40. SOUTH CAROLINA
The Last Frontier • Rebecca Flanders
41. SOUTH DAKOTA
For Old Times' Sake • Kathleen Eagle
42. TENNESSEE
To Love a Dreamer • Ruth Langan
43. TEXAS
For the Love of Mike • Candace Schuler
44. UTAH
To Tame the Hunter • Stephanie James
45. VERMONT
Finders Keepers • Carla Neggers
46. VIRGINIA
The Devlin Dare • Cathy Gillen Thacker
47. WASHINGTON
The Waiting Game • Jayne Ann Krentz
48. WEST VIRGINIA
All in the Family • Heather Graham Pozzessere
49. WISCONSIN
Starstruck • Anne McAllister
50. WYOMING
Special Touches • Sharon Brondos

CANDACE SCHULER

For the Love of Mike

Harlequin Books

TORONTO • NEW YORK • LONDON
AMSTERDAM • PARIS • SYDNEY • HAMBURG
STOCKHOLM • ATHENS • TOKYO • MILAN
MADRID • WARSAW • BUDAPEST • AUCKLAND

With thanks to Jan Korkamas
of Limousines By Jan

HARLEQUIN ENTERPRISES LTD.
225 Duncan Mill Road, Don Mills,
Ontario, Canada M3B 3K9

FOR THE LOVE OF MIKE

1

"HEY, MIKE." The soft female voice, pitched to carry, finally penetrated through the noise of the revving engine. "Mike, could you come here a minute? We've got a problem."

The slim young woman who had been so addressed lifted her head at the sound of her name. Seeing her secretary hovering halfway between the service bay and the open door to the connecting offices, she signaled to the mechanic to turn off the engine. Straightening up, Mike reached for a nearby rag to wipe some of the grease smears off her hands.

She had been christened Michaelann at birth, a melding of her parents' names, but no one had called her anything but Mike for as long as she could remember. The nickname had suited her as a child. She had been a rough-and-tumble tomboy whose favorite playmates were her two older brothers and their rowdy friends. During her teen years she had liked nothing better than to tinker with the farm tractors and the family car. Since she still liked nothing better than to tinker with cars, it was not surprising that the nickname had followed her into womanhood.

At twenty-four, with her own limousine service and almost two dozen full-time employees on her payroll,

Michaelann Frazer still gave the impression of a wild young colt: all long legs, supple well-toned arms and boyishly slim hips, topped by a short unruly mop of light gingery curls. She was covered from head to toe by a blanket of pale reddish freckles, like a dappled roan horse, and her eyes were large and green and looked at the world with a lively curiosity and a sharp business sense.

"What is it, Vicki?" she asked. Her voice was low and husky with just the barest trace of a Texas drawl. She tossed the greasy rag aside as she strode across the concrete floor of the garage. "One of the drivers giving you trouble?"

Blue-eyed blond-haired doll-like Vicki shook her tousled head. "Not exactly," she said in tones of dire foreboding as she pushed open the door and stepped back inside the small tidy front office of Unicorn Limousine Service.

It wasn't plush, but it was neat and comfortable. The carpet was dark gray, a heavy-duty industrial weave meant to last, and the furniture—two modern-looking burgundy armchairs with a chrome-legged table between them, a gray metal desk and a four-drawer filing cabinet—was sturdy and serviceable. The wall behind Vicki's desk was painted to match the chairs and sported a large stylized rendering of a rearing unicorn with the words Unicorn Limousine Service arced in a half circle above it and the legend A Magical Experience below. The other three pale gray walls were lined with silver-framed posters of great classic cars.

"Take that thing off before you come in here," Vicki warned, waving a manicured hand at Mike's grease-smeared baggy blue coverall. "I don't want grease all over my nice clean office."

Obligingly Mike unzipped the offending garment, and stepped out of it to reveal the gentle curves of her unbound breasts beneath a checkered shirt. Suddenly the name Mike was not quite the perfect fit that it had been just a minute ago.

She hung the dirty coverall on a hook just outside the office door so she could find it again. "So," she said, flinging herself into one of the low-slung chairs in front of Vicki's desk. She hooked one long, lean leg over the chair's arm. "What's the problem?"

"Cheryl just called in," Vicki informed her boss. "She was on her way out to DFW to pick up a Mr.—" she glanced at the schedule book on her desk "—Mr. Wingate of Wingate Industries. But she's had a little fender bender and—"

Mike bolted upright, and her sneakered feet hit the carpeted floor with a thud. "Which car is she driving?" she demanded, thinking instantly of the newest addition to her fleet, a classic 1939 Rolls-Royce Silver Wraith. She could almost picture it, its beautiful sloping fenders crumpled and broken, marooned by the side of the highway. It would cost a small fortune to repair. A small fortune that she didn't have at the moment because she had put every penny she could spare into buying the car in the first place.

"Relax, it's not your new toy. Bonnie has that today for some society wedding."

Mike sank back into the depths of the chair, relieved. Then she sat up straight again. "Is Cheryl all right?" she asked guiltily, knowing that it should have been her first question.

"She's fine," Vicki assured her. "Just a small bump on her forehead where she hit the steering wheel."

"Anybody else hurt?"

"She thinks the other driver has a broken arm, but they have to take him for X-rays to be sure."

"And the car? Which one is it?" Mike closed her eyes, putting a hand to her forehead. "Give it to me straight. How bad?"

Vicki grinned. Mike worried more about her precious cars than other women did about their children. "It's one of the standard factory Caddys. All the damage is on the driver's side. Crumpled fender, broken headlight. Some bozo tried to go straight in a left-turn-only lane."

Mike nodded and heaved herself to her feet. It wasn't so bad, after all. No one had been seriously injured, and it didn't sound as if the car was too badly damaged. Thank God, it was a standard American model and not one of her fancy custom stretches, or worse, one of her three foreign classics. At least parts would be easy to get, if not exactly inexpensive.

"Well, you know what to do," she instructed her secretary. "Get hold of our insurance agent and start arguing with him over the cost of the repairs." She headed for the door to the garage.

"Hey, boss." Vicki's soft voice called her back. "That's not all."

"Not all?" Mike stopped in the doorway without turning around. A cold chill ran down her spine. "Is Cheryl the bozo who made the wrong turn?" she asked, thoughts of sky-high insurance premiums dancing through her head.

Vicki snickered. "No."

"The other driver wants to sue us, anyway?"

"No." Vicki waited patiently for Mike to turn around. "You have to go pick up Mr. Wingate," she said, smiling.

"*I* have to go?" It had been a while since Mike had done any chauffeuring herself. When you owned the company, she thought, you didn't have to. She much preferred to fool around under the hood. Besides, being obliged to conform to the fifty-five mile an hour speed limit put a decided cramp in her driving style. "Why?"

"Because there's nobody else available, that's why. Cheryl's had that accident, Bonnie's working that society wedding." Vicki's pink-tipped finger ran down the schedule book. "Karen, Jan and Dottie are all booked. In fact, there are *three* weddings today. It's June," she reminded Mike. "So everyone is—"

"Never mind." Mike held up a slim hand to ward off the rest. "I get the general idea." She sighed in mock weariness. "Who, where and what time?"

"Mr. Devlin Wingate, American Airlines, Terminal 3E, flight 52 from Houston in—" she glanced at her watch "—exactly twenty-two minutes."

"Twenty-two minutes! Well, why didn't you say so?"

"I just did," Vicki said, but Mike was already out the door and headed at a run toward the drivers' locker room.

She slowed her flight halfway across the garage. "Have someone do a predrive check on the stretch Caddy," she instructed, flicking a hand in the direction of the long silver car parked along one side of the garage. "I haven't got time." She disappeared into the locker room.

Twenty-two minutes! Even if she left right now, she'd never make it, not without breaking the speed limit, anyway. Although she thought nothing of doing just that in her own personal car, a restored 1947 MG with a built-in radar detector, it wasn't something she liked to do behind the wheel of one of her stately Caddys.

Quickly she unbuttoned her yellow checkered shirt and shimmied out of her jeans, kicking her sneakers off as she did so. It took ten minutes under the shower with a bar of Lava soap to get the grease and perspiration off her, and a brisk two minutes with a rough terry towel to dry and "style" her short baby-fine hair. Banging open her locker, she yanked out her seldom used uniform and stepped into it, adjusting the material to lie flat over the curve of her breasts.

It was cut like the classic chauffeur's uniform, the one that was featured in all the old movies on the late show, but instead of being made of heavy black wool it was cut from a lightweight blend in a soft pearl gray that was better suited to the Texas climate. The tailored slacks had a burgundy stripe down each leg, and there were two matching stripes on the cuff of each coat sleeve. The double row of silver buttons down the front of the jacket had tiny rearing unicorns etched on them. They had been specially made to match her company logo—as had the unicorns that replaced the hood ornaments on all of Mike's cars, even her beautiful Silver Wraith.

Hastily Mike applied her only cosmetics, a quick application of mascara on her pale lashes to keep her from looking, as one of her brothers had once said, "like a rabbit that just woke up," and a touch of clear gloss to keep her lips from drying out in the Texas heat. She didn't take the time to see the fresh beauty of the face that stared back at her: not the wide green eyes with the unusual flecks of gold in the irises, not the full sexy mouth with its ready smile, nor the finely chiseled jaw with its firm chin.

All Mike saw, when she allowed herself to see anything, were lashes that needed mascara to be visible, a mouth that was too wide, a chin that made her look stubborn, and freckles. To Mike, those freckles automatically barred her from any possible claim she might have otherwise had to good looks.

She set the jaunty chauffeur's cap on her head, haphazardly stuffing her ginger curls under it, and adjusted the brim so that the tiny silver unicorn etched on the bill was set squarely over her forehead. Then she stepped into a pair of low-heeled gray pumps, smoothed a pair of matching gray gloves over her hands and was ready. Six more minutes had passed. She hurried out to the long silver Caddy at a trot, threw a hurried "Thanks, Dave" to the mechanic who had done the predrive check, and roared out into the busy Dallas traffic.

Crowding the speed limit as much as she dared without a radar detector, she mentally reviewed the too-little time left to her before her passenger's plane got in. If luck was with her today, she thought, if the plane was just ten or fifteen minutes late . . . but luck wasn't with her. Flight 52 had already arrived—ten minutes early.

Knowing it was too late to connect with her passenger at the gate, Mike hurried to the baggage claim area, her white plastic message-board held high over her head in an effort to locate him. Unicorn Limousines it said across the top in bold letters; the name Devlin Wingate was scrawled in grease pencil beneath it. She circled the baggage carousel four times, her anxious eyes scanning the crowd, but no one admitted to being Devlin Wingate. For a moment she debated making use of the airport paging system to locate him but then decided to check back at the car first. Maybe *he* had gone outside to look for *her*, she thought hopefully as she headed back outside at a trot.

As she exited the automatic doors, Mike saw a man in a tan felt cowboy hat, shiny brown cowboy boots and a rumpled business suit standing on the curb next to the big silver car. He held a briefcase in one hand and a battered, much-traveled suitcase sat on the pavement beside him. *Ah, there he is*, Mike thought, relieved. It was no wonder he hadn't been in the baggage claim area; he had only one carryon suitcase. She fixed a bright welcoming smile on her face as she came up behind him.

"Mr. Wingate?" she said, tapping him lightly on the shoulder.

He turned and looked at her blankly.

"Are you Mr. Wingate?" she asked again, but the man was already shaking his head no.

"No, he's not," said a voice from behind her. "I am."

"Oh, I'm sorry. Please . . . please excuse me," Mike stammered, trying to apologize to both men at once. She turned and looked up into the face of the man who had spoken. Her first thought was that it was one of the most handsome faces she had ever seen. At least, she amended immediately, it would be if it weren't marred by an irate frown.

Even with the frown, though, it was a clean-edged aristocratic face, all angles and planes, with a sharp, straight nose and a firm, chiseled jawline that hinted at more stubbornness than even Mike possessed. His eyes were gray and they were fringed, she noted enviously, with long dark lashes. His brows were dark, too, twin slashes above his eyes, drawn together now by impatience. His hair was a rich blue-black, with a soft wave where it was brushed away from his forehead. It was impossible to tell anything about his mouth at the moment except that he was badly out of temper.

He was much younger than she had expected a man in his position to be: men with companies named after them should be at least fifty, she thought crossly. This man couldn't have been more than thirty-three or thirty-four. On top of that, he didn't look like a dyed-in-the-wool Texan from Houston, either. He looked almost European, she thought, but maybe that was just because of the very European cut of his elegant navy suit.

"Are you Mr. Devlin Wingate?" she asked, just to be sure.

"Yes." He nodded curtly, his eyes resting impatiently on the big silver car by the curb.

"I'm sorry to be late, sir," she began pleasantly. "There was an unavoidable emergency and—"

"Spare me the excuses, please," he interrupted, reaching for the car's door handle before she could do it for him. He tossed his briefcase onto the plushly upholstered back seat and slid into the air-conditioned coolness after it. "The rest of my bags are still in the terminal. Please get them." He thrust the claim checks through the open door without looking at her. "Gray leather with metal luggage tags."

Automatically Mike reached to take the claim checks from his outstretched fingers. His gesture had exposed the correct one and a half inches of crisp white shirt cuff, fastened, she noted, with small silver-and-blue enameled cuff links instead of the more usual buttons. She also couldn't help but notice how well kept his hands were. Much better cared for than hers, she thought wryly. They were long-fingered elegant hands, as tanned as his face and dusted with a sprinkling of fine black hairs across the backs. His nails and cuticles were smooth and shiny, as if they were professionally manicured on a regular basis.

Dismissing him and his well-kept hands with a philosophical shrug, Mike turned back toward the terminal building. The automatic doors slid open as she approached them, and a blast of cold air hit her in the face. It felt wonderful and she paused for the slightest moment to savor the coolness. Then she clutched the claim checks more tightly in her hand and headed for the baggage carousel.

He had four pieces of luggage: a garment bag, an overnighter and two large suitcases, with a designer logo stamped into a corner of each soft leather piece. More luggage than she'd take on a month's vacation, Mike thought as she slung the strap of the garment bag over her shoulder. She wedged the smallest suitcase under one arm and then clasped the other two firmly, one in each hand. Thus burdened, she waddled out to the limousine.

The rear door was still wide open, affording Mike a clear view of the man in the back seat. His dark head was bent as he looked at something in his lap. Business papers probably, she decided. He was reading them as if he hadn't the slightest idea that she was just outside the car, struggling with his luggage. Not that she expected any help, of course, but still . . . he could have at least acknowledged her presence, couldn't he? The fact that he didn't piqued her temper in some indefinable way.

She put everything down on the curb and popped open the trunk. He didn't look up. She lifted his fancy leather suitcases into the carpeted spanking-clean interior and slammed the lid with more force than was strictly necessary. There was no reaction from the man in the back seat.

Mike shrugged and went around to the open door. She hesitated for a moment, her fingers on the handle as she debated whether or not to give her passenger the usual spiel about the car's features. "This is the control for the television. Push this to operate the sunroof . . ." was how it usually went. She decided not to. Devlin Wingate looked like a man who was already more than a little familiar with the inside of a limousine. Besides, he still hadn't glanced up from those papers he was reading.

With a practiced little flick of her wrist, Mike closed the passenger door and circled the hood to the driver's side of the car. Sliding into the cool, plush interior of the long silver Cadillac, she inserted the key into the ignition. The big car came quietly to life. Mike smiled to herself. How she loved the sound of a well-tuned engine.

"Are you charging me by the minute?" asked her passenger. Mike could almost feel the steel of his voice pierce the back of her head, despite the pleasant tone he assumed.

She stiffened in her seat, and her hands, in their soft gray gloves, curled around the steering wheel. "I beg your pardon?"

"And so you should," he said, his words as sharp as his clean-edged jawline.

"Sir?" Mike said politely.

"I am not accustomed to waiting," he informed her. "I don't like it."

Well, who does? she thought.

"And I am also not accustomed to giving an order more than once."

And I'm not accustomed to taking them, she thought, staring straight ahead. Besides, he hadn't given her any order.

There was a loud sigh from the back seat. "Would it be too much trouble for you to drive me to my destination?" he said, his voice exaggeratedly polite. "Please," he added very softly, but it was an order, nonetheless.

"No trouble at all, sir," Mike replied sweetly. "As soon as you tell me where you'd like me to take you." She looked into the rearview mirror, and her vivid green eyes met her passenger's. She knew where she'd *like* to take him.

Their gazes locked for a few seconds, and then his eyes widened in surprise. "You're a woman," he stated flatly.

No kidding, thought Mike. "Yes, sir," she said, falsely polite. She held his gaze in the mirror and, goaded by the incredulous look in his eyes, her next words came out a bit sharper than she had intended. "Do you have any objections to that?"

"Not as long as you can do your job." He paused for a split second before delivering the final blow. "You *can* drive this thing, can't you?" he said.

Mike didn't reply. Instead she pulled the big stretch Caddy smoothly away from the curb and, taking an educated guess, headed toward the north exit gates of the airport. Most of the newer high-rise hotels were in North Dallas, and he looked to her like a man who stayed at only the most modern, most plush facilities available.

She heard the hum of the glass partition as it rose into place behind her head and glanced into the rearview mirror again. Devlin Wingate was bent over the papers in his lap . . . and he still hadn't told her where he wanted to go.

It would serve him right, she thought, *if I just drove around for a couple of hours.*

Devlin Wingate felt Mike's eyes on him, but he continued to idly peruse the papers before him. He was perfectly aware that he hadn't told her where he wanted to go yet, but he needed to get his temper under control first.

He wasn't usually rude to the people who worked for him, even if they were only temporarily in that capacity. In fact, if asked twenty minutes ago, he would have said that he was never rude to those not in a position to be rude right back to him. Curt, sometimes, he admitted to himself, and perhaps even a trifle abrupt on occasion but never downright rude.

Obviously he was tired and irritable and in no condition to keep a curb on his tongue. Mémé Lucie had been right. He should have accepted her invitation to spend the weekend at her house outside New Orleans after this last leg of his cross-country trip instead of rushing home to close the negotiations on the Dallas land development deal.

Of course, he thought, trying to rationalize his behavior, it could be that there was something about the driver that just rubbed him the wrong way.

A wry grin curved his lips, softening the sharp planes of his handsome face as he thought of those wide green eyes staring back at him in the mirror. He'd certainly like to have her try rubbing him the right way, he thought, surprising himself.

She wasn't his usual type, not with that long, boyish body, and no hips or bust to speak of—at least not that he'd noticed. Devlin liked his women with a little more meat on their bones; it gave a man something to hold on to in bed. Although, he mused, you could never tell what might be under that chauffeur's uniform.

He eyed the soft, wispy curls that escaped from under the chauffeur's cap she wore. She was a redhead, he realized, wondering why he hadn't noticed that immediately. He had always been partial to redheads, even freckled ones. *Especially* freckled ones, he amended with a slight grin.

Ever since that momentous occasion when his high school steady, Amy Griffen, let him "go all the way," he had had a soft spot for freckled women. Amy, with her flaming carrot top, had been covered with them.

Was this impudent, skinny young woman covered with them, too? he wondered, feeling a sudden urge to find out for himself.

"You must be more tired than you realize, Dev," he said softly, his firm, sensual mouth curving in a smile of self-deprecation. It wasn't like him to indulge in sexual fantasies about strange women, especially not skinny young women who drove cars for a living.

Suddenly he could almost hear Mémé Lucie's soft Louisiana Cajun patois. "Snob," said his grandmother clearly.

With a sigh, Devlin reached toward the control panel to his left and pushed the button that would lower the glass partition between the seats. He intended to apologize for his rudeness and to give the driver the address of his condominium.

"Yes, sir?" Mike said before the window was all the way down. Her eyes went automatically to the rearview mirror, meeting his in silent inquiry.

"I'm . . ." Devlin's mind went blank. Lord, what fantastic eyes, he thought. At the moment they were as wide and inquisitive as a startled doe's, as clear and fresh as a spring rain, as green as new grass; a man could get lost in those eyes.

Mike returned his stare for a second or two, feeling the intensity of his gaze all the way to her toes, and then jerked her eyes away from the mirror and refocused her gaze on the road ahead. "Did you want something, sir?" she asked pointedly, trying valiantly to ignore the heat of the blush that was rising up from under the collar of her uniform.

Forcing his voice to sound crisply impersonal, he reeled off the address of an expensive high-rise building in the Turtle Creek area of Dallas. Then he pushed the button in the control panel again, raising the glass between them. He didn't even remember that he had intended to apologize.

What a strange young woman, he thought again, choosing for the moment to ignore the strange way *he* was reacting to her. She had the figure of a teenage boy, the eyes of Eve, and if he wasn't mistaken, as many freckles as the first girl he had ever loved. He wondered again what she looked like under her uniform.

He shook his head, laughing silently at himself. "Forget it, Dev," he said softly. "She's not your type." Resolutely he bent his head over the papers in his lap and began to read.

Fuming, Mike gripped the steering wheel with her gloved hands. The nerve of the man, she thought, sneaking glances at his lowered head in the rearview mirror. Who did he think he was, snapping out orders as if he were the lord of the manor or something? And the way he had looked at her was unnerving.

Just what had he been looking at so intently, she wondered, briefly meeting her own gaze in the mirror. She saw nothing unusual staring back at her, just an ordinary pair of green eyes, surrounded by a sea of pale freckles. She shrugged, focusing on the road ahead. Maybe she reminded him of someone he knew. Or, more likely, maybe he just couldn't believe that she was really a woman.

Suddenly Mike's train of thought was interrupted as the steering wheel pulled abruptly to the right. She was immediately alert, feeling the movement of the car through her hands on the wheel and the seat of her pants. There was an odd thumping sound coming from the region of the right front tire. It could only be one thing, she realized with a sinking feeling in the pit of her stomach—a flat. Great, that was just what she needed!

Someone, she promised herself, holding the wheel steady as she eased up on the gas pedal, was going to have a lot of explaining to do when she got back to the garage. These cars, including the tires, were supposed to be in tip-top condition. Skillfully she maneuvered across three lanes of highway traffic and pulled into the breakdown lane. Only then did she spare a thought for the man in the back seat.

He looked up as she pulled to a stop, and the glass partition began to descend again. His eyebrows, she noticed, were pulled together in a frown.

Didn't he have any other expression, she wondered.

"What's the problem?" He sounded annoyed.

Mike shifted the car into park and turned the engine off, but left the key in the ignition so that the electrical system would still operate. "I'm sorry," she said without turning around. Her glance met his in the mirror again and then skittered away. Looking into his eyes did strange things to her insides. "I think we've got a flat."

"Terrific." The word was expelled with a breath of impatience. "I'm already running behind schedule," he began, and Mike steeled herself, waiting for the explosion that was sure to follow.

From what she had observed so far, she had the feeling that Devlin Wingate was a man with a low boiling point. He certainly hadn't made any effort to control his temper up till now, she thought. But there was a silence from the back seat.

"Has this thing got a phone?" His voice sounded resigned.

"A phone?" It took Mike a minute to realize that he was actually going to be reasonable. "Yes, sir. Just open that little door below the television there." She set the emergency brake, then twisted around, half leaning over the seat back to show him. Their hands touched as they both reached for the phone at the same time. Mike's eyes flew up to his face and she froze, her hand still covering his.

Her first thought was that she was glad she was wearing gloves. Otherwise he would be able to feel the way her palm had suddenly begun to perspire. Her second thought was to wish that she had been wearing sunglasses as well.

His eyes, on a level with hers, were a clear slate gray with the tiniest rim of black around the irises. They gleamed like polished bits of smoky quartz, reminding her of the shiny "steelie" marbles that she had played with as a child. They were also, she thought, far too close to her own! If he blinked, his lashes would probably brush against her cheeks.

Mike gulped back a sigh, her own lashes fluttering slightly.

"I think I can handle it from here," he said very softly. Mike heard the faintest thread of an accent in his voice. Something not entirely Texan, she thought again, giving a tiny nod of her head in agreement with his words. Her eyes, however, were still locked with his, and she seemed unable to move.

"Miss—" Devlin glanced down at her jacket, looking for a name tag. There wasn't one. "Miss . . . ?"

"Frazer," she said huskily, blushing faintly as his eyes seemed to probe through the covering of her uniform. "Mike—Michaelann Augusta Frazer," she corrected herself hastily, telling him, for God alone knew what reason, her horrible, ridiculous full name.

"Well, Miss Michaelann Augusta Frazer," he said, gently removing her hand from his so that he could get at the telephone. "Thank you for your assistance, but I think I can handle it from here." Then, for the first time, he smiled at her.

His gray eyes crinkled up at the corners, sending a scattering of fine spidery lines chasing into his temples. His lips relaxed and parted, revealing a row of strong white teeth, startlingly bright against the tan of his skin.

Mike was entranced. Tentatively she smiled back, her full rosy lips curving upward to reveal a deep dimple in her right cheek. The upward movement seemed to set her freckles dancing all over her face.

They held their positions, smiling at each other for seemingly endless seconds, and then suddenly Mike realized where she was and who she was with. Her smile faded instantly. This man was a client! And a far too attractive one at that.

"I have to get that tire changed," she said abruptly, turning away. She popped the trunk release, speaking to him over her shoulder as she pretended to watch the passing cars to make sure it was safe to open the door. "Usually I'd call the garage and have another limo dispatched to come and pick you up," she explained nervously. "But we're a bit shorthanded just now and—"

There was a break in the traffic, and Mike quickly broke off what she was saying to take advantage of it. "It will only take a few minutes," she assured him as she slid out of the car. Pulling off her gloves, she scurried around to the trunk for the jack and spare tire.

Devlin sat with the telephone in his hand for a few seconds, a speculative, somewhat amused look on his face as he watched her efficiently set the jack and begin to raise the right front corner of the car. He had a brief moment of chivalry, wondering if he should get out and offer to help her in spite of the damage such an action might have on the cleanliness of his suit. It was awfully hot out there, upward of ninety-five degrees, and she *was* a woman—and a fairly skinny one at that.

But that impulse was abruptly stilled as Mike straightened up. She lifted her cap from her head, spilling soft gingery curls over her forehead and neck, and dabbed at her face with the sleeve of her uniform. Then she set the cap on the shiny hood of the car and began to unbutton her jacket.

Devlin held his breath, waiting. Mike slipped the unbuttoned jacket down her arms, folded it neatly in half and laid it across the hood next to her cap. Then she went back to work.

Not so skinny as she seemed at first, Devlin thought, focusing intently on the way the material of her short-sleeved white cotton shirt clung to her. She wasn't busty, but she was braless, and the two middle buttons gaped a bit as her arms pumped up and down on the jack, affording a teasing glimpse of the inner curve of her breasts. Devlin sat up a little straighter.

No, not skinny at all, he decided. Slender was the proper word; lithe and willowy. Like the young Diana of Greek mythology, her body was sleek and strong and gracefully athletic. Her breasts were small, with prominent little nipples that pushed against the front of her shirt. Her arms, bared from the midbicep down, were firm and well toned, with narrow, almost fragile-looking wrists. And, he noted with a grin, as covered with freckles as her face.

"Maybe she's your type, after all, Dev, ol' boy," he said to himself as he began to punch the numbers on the telephone.

He made his call quickly, watching Mike all the while, and then settled back in the seat, his arms folded across his chest, his head tilted as he gave her his undivided attention.

She had finished jacking the car up and was crouched beside the fender, the top of her ginger head the only thing visible as she struggled with the lug nuts on the wheel. He heard a muffled curse and a dull thud as, presumably, her hand hit the side of the car in frustration.

He lowered the side window. "Need any help?" he said solicitously, smiling at her. He made no move to get out of the car.

"No, thanks. I can manage." Mike threw the words over her shoulder as she continued to struggle with the lug wrench. "You'd just get your fancy suit dirty," she added under her breath. Not to mention getting grease under those manicured nails, she thought, and messing up that salon-styled hair.

She gave a savage yank on the lug wrench, putting all her weight behind it. It came loose suddenly, surprising her, and she rocked back on her heels, sitting down hard on the graveled surface of the road.

"Sure you don't need any help?" The smile had widened into a teasing grin.

Mike looked up at him, her green eyes narrowing as she took in the expression on his face. It was a definite improvement over the frown, but she didn't like being laughed at, especially not by good-looking men in expensive European suits.

She directed a puff of breath upward at the curls clinging to her damp forehead before answering. "I'm sure," she said, pushing herself back to her feet. "I've already loosened the rest of them."

Quickly, as if to prove the truth of her words, she unscrewed the remaining lugs with her fingers and dropped them into the nearby hubcap. Then she wiggled the tire, eased it off the wheel and straightened up. Devlin Wingate was still watching her through the open window.

"Mr. Wingate, I think you might want to close that window," she suggested sweetly, a dangerous look in her eyes. "Otherwise all the cool air inside the car will just rush right out into this heat, won't it?"

Devlin took the hint, another delighted grin crossing his face, and raised the window into place. Mike tried to ignore him, but she was still very much aware of the fact that he was staring at her through the smoked glass. She couldn't see inside, of course, but she knew he could see out—she could *feel* his eyes on her. As a result, when she lifted the spare tire into place, her hands were not as steady as they usually were.

"Dammit," she swore softly as she struggled to fit the wheel onto the hub. Why on earth was that man watching her like that? It was nerve-racking, to say the least.

She could understand it if she looked like Vicki—*she* had the kind of face and figure that any man would turn around to gape at. But what man would want to stare at a tall, skinny woman with freckles, especially one that he had mistaken for a boy? He must have a screw loose somewhere in that aristocratic head of his, she decided.

The tire finally slipped into place, and Mike crouched down on her heels to replace the lug nuts, first snugging them down with her fingers and then finally tightening them with quick hard twists of the wrench. She fitted the hubcap on, banging it firmly into place with the heel of her hand, and then quickly lowered the car to the ground.

Maybe he just liked to watch other people sweat, she thought, shooting a glance at the window out of the corner of her eye as she rolled the flat tire back toward the rear of the car. Maybe it gave him a sense of smug superiority to watch other people perform manual labor. Who knew?

Oh, well, she decided, fitting everything back into the trunk, it didn't matter, anyway. What mattered was getting him to his condo and out of her hair.

She slammed the trunk lid shut and walked around the right side of the car to retrieve her cap and jacket.

The last thing she wanted to do in this heat was put them back on, but rules were rules, especially when she was the one who had made them. She couldn't expect her drivers to follow them if she didn't.

Besides, she admitted grudgingly, she felt almost indecently exposed with the thin cotton shirt sticking to her damp skin and her passenger watching her like a hawk.

She plopped the cap on her head, unmindful of the gingery curls that stuck to her forehead and neck, and slipped into the long-sleeved chauffeur's jacket, buttoning it up as she moved around the front of the car to the driver's side. The cool air-conditioned interior was a welcome balm to her heat-flushed damp skin, but she wasted no time in savoring the feeling. She released the emergency brake, her eyes on the side mirror as she waited for an opening in the highway traffic, and turned the key in the ignition, gently revving the engine to life.

"You did that pretty quickly," said her passenger. His voice was very near and she realized that he had shifted across to the seat that butted against the back of hers. "Was changing tires part of your chauffeur's training?" he asked lazily.

That thread of an accent teased at her again, but she still couldn't place it. Despite his elegant Gallic looks, it definitely wasn't French. "Yes, Mr. Wingate, it was," she said stiffly, her eyes fastened on the side mirror. *And just what are you doing now,* she wondered, feeling a tiny shiver along the nape of her neck at his nearness. First he was as rude and abrasive as some English duke, and now he was acting like he wanted to make friends with the hired help.

"Did it take you very long to learn?" he asked then. He wasn't really interested in her answer, but he *was* interested in hearing her speak again. She sounded, he thought, like a young Lauren Bacall might have sounded if she'd been from Texas. Hers was a smoky voice, a bedroom voice, and it sent shivers racing down his spine.

Devlin knew he should just sit back and forget this absurd attraction, but he couldn't. It was too strong, and although he would never have admitted it, Devlin wasn't the kind of man to deny himself something he wanted—even if it wasn't going to be good for him.

"Did what take me very long?" Mike said, trying to pretend that all her attention was focused on the fast-moving traffic. "Learning to change a tire?" Her eyes shifted from the side mirror to the rearview one, and when she couldn't see him, she turned her head slightly to glance over her shoulder.

He was sitting with his right elbow propped up on her seat back, his chin resting in his palm. There was a look of absorbed interest on his face as his eyes roamed over her. He smiled lazily as he caught her eye. Mike's head whipped forward again, and she could feel the heat of a blush begin to rise up to color her throat.

"Not just changing a tire," he said. She caught a blur of movement out of the corner of her eye as he made an arcing motion with his free hand. "But everything that you had to learn about being a chauffeur."

"No, not long—*Mr. Wingate!*" Mike's head snapped around again as she felt him run the tip of one finger down the side of her neck. She glared at him, her wide green eyes reduced to narrowed slits.

Not a startled doe any longer, he thought. She looks like a cornered, angry cat now. Diana the huntress. Devlin felt his pulses quicken.

"I would very much appreciate it if you would sit back and try not to distract me while I'm driving," she said indignantly, the heat of her blush fusing all her freckles into one solid mass of pink.

Devlin grinned at her, unabashed. "Do I distract you?" he asked, a note of hope in his voice. He looked at her with a lazily seductive, teasing light in his gray eyes.

"Yes!" Mike said furiously. She turned forward again, finding him much too close for comfort. "The same way a fly would be distracting if it were buzzing around in the car."

With that, she stomped on the gas pedal, shooting them out into the flow of traffic. Devlin shifted back onto the rear bench seat, propelled partly by the sudden forward motion of the car. She could hear his soft laughter over the roar of the engine.

Of all the arrogant, smug, *infuriating* men she had ever met, this one really took the cake! The sooner she dropped him off, the better. And if he said one more word to her on the way, she vowed, she would stop the car and throw him out!

But wisely Devlin didn't say another word until they pulled to a stop in front of an impressive high-rise condominium in Turtle Creek.

Mike jumped out of the car as if she had been propelled by a slingshot and hurried around to open the trunk. She left the task of opening the door for her passenger to the uniformed doorman who hurried out of the building to perform that service.

"Mr. Wingate, what a pleasure it is to have you home again," Mike heard the doorman say as she shifted the luggage from the trunk of the Cadillac to sit on the curb, but her real attention was focused on the tall, leggy young woman who had followed him out to the car.

Her curling shoulder-length hair was glossy black, her eyes were dark, her mouth was soft and red, and her skin was smooth and golden brown, as if she spent a good deal of time lounging by a pool. She stood impatiently on the curb, her hands stuffed into the pockets of an ecru sundress that managed to look both casual and expensive, shifting her slight weight from one foot to the other as she waited for Devlin to give her his full attention.

It was obvious from the way she looked at him that Devlin was someone she adored. And from the expression on Devlin's face when he finally turned to greet her, it was apparent that he was pretty fond of her, too.

"Trisha, honey, it's good to see you," he said, bending down to kiss her proffered cheek. "You must have been waiting by the door," he added with a lift of his eyebrows at the way she had come hurrying out to meet him. "Miss me?"

"Not a bit," she teased, squeezing his arm affectionately. "I'm just hungry, that's all. Even after you called, Mother insisted on waiting lunch until you got here, and I'm practically starving," she said, her voice girlishly accusing and barely tinged with a soft Texas twang. "What kept you so long?"

"Oh, this and that," Devlin answered noncommittally. He glanced over at Mike with a teasing light in his gray eyes.

But Mike wasn't looking at him. She was hurrying around the back of the car toward the driver's side, intent on getting away from the disturbing Mr. Wingate and his beautiful companion as fast as humanly possible.

"Miss Frazer, your tip." Devlin's voice halted her as she put her hand on the door handle.

"No, thank you, sir," Mike said primly, touching her hand smartly to the brim of her cap in a mock salute. Her eyes met his over the top of the car. "And there will be no charge for the ride from the airport, either, because of the inconvenience I've caused you." She ducked into the car before he could answer and drove away without once looking in the rearview mirror.

2

MIKE DIDN'T LOOK UP as the door of her office creaked open. She was intent on the papers spread out in front of her on the desk. They summarized her current financial condition, which, after scraping up the cash to buy out her brother Billy Ray's twenty-percent share of Unicorn Limousine and taking out the loan to pay for the Silver Wraith, was not as good as she would have liked it to be. It was the first time she'd been in this much debt since starting the business, and she didn't like the feeling. Not one bit. The fact that the debt was necessary—and had been planned for—mattered not a whit. She still didn't like it.

"Mike?" Vicki's voice was hesitant. Her expertly tousled blond head was the only part of her visible around the edge of the door.

"One second." Mike marked her place in the column of figures with the tip of one finger, then raised her eyes, silently inviting her secretary to come in. "What is it?"

Vicki stepped into the office and closed the door, leaning back against it with a rather dreamy look in her big blue eyes. "There's a man here to see you."

Must be a good-looking one, Mike thought, judging from the silly expression on her secretary's face. "Who?" she asked.

Vicki sighed and then seemed to shake herself back to reality. "You're not going to be pleased," she warned, absently picking at a piece of nonexistent fuzz on the skirt of her soft pink dress as she spoke.

"Why am I not going to be pleased? Who is it?"

Vicki tilted her head, a considering look in her blue eyes. "Devlin Wingate."

"Wingate!" Mike half rose out of her chair, a look of something like alarm on her freckled face. She sank back down. "Damn," she swore softly. "I already told him that the answer is no."

"Yes, I know." Vicki couldn't help but grin at her employer's apparent distress. "But it seems Mr. Wingate isn't the kind of man who takes no for an answer."

"Or maybe he just doesn't understand the word," Mike snapped.

"Maybe," Vicki agreed easily. "He probably hasn't heard it often enough to become familiar with it." She grinned again. "He certainly wouldn't hear it from me, that's for sure. I could never say no to a man who looks like that. Those eyes of his are incredible. And he's so—" Vicki paused briefly, searching for a word "—so elegant."

Mike snorted with disgust. "You have absolutely no taste," she admonished the other woman, trying very hard not to remember those eyes, that sartorial elegance, for herself. "And he is, too, going to hear it from you. Because you're going to go out there—" she waved toward the closed door "—right now and tell him I'm not here."

"He already *knows* you're here, Mike."

"Tell him I'm busy, then."

"He told me to tell you that he'd wait if you were busy."

"Fine. Let him wait." Mike picked up her pencil and bent her head over the papers on her desk as if the matter were settled.

"He also said to tell you that he's prepared to wait all day, if necessary. He means it, too," Vicki informed her gleefully. "He had me send his taxi away." She tilted her head again, causing a tangled sheaf of blond hair to topple forward over one perfectly made-up eye. She shook it back with a practiced toss of her head. "Did something happen on the way back from the airport the other day?" she asked curiously. "You were kind of, ummm, flushed when you got back."

"I had to change a tire, remember?" Mike said, her head still bent to the papers on her desk. "And it was over ninety-five degrees. Who wouldn't be flushed?"

"Maybe." Vicki still wasn't convinced. "But are you *sure* something else didn't happen?"

Mike's head snapped up. "Like what?" she asked, exasperation and wariness in her voice.

"Like something romantic, maybe? He looks like the kind of man who wouldn't think twice about making a pass at an attractive woman."

"He didn't even know I was a woman at first!" Mike interjected and then could have bitten her tongue when she saw the knowing look on her secretary's face. "Besides," she added defensively, twisting a pencil around in her hands, "I'm not an attractive woman. At least," she continued as Vicki opened her mouth to disagree, "not his type of attractive." Mike ran an assessing eye up and down her secretary's shapely form. "*You're* his type."

"Nope." Vicki shook her head, grinning. "He didn't even try to look down the front of my dress." She pointed a pink-tipped finger at Mike. "It's you he's after. Why else would he be so insistent about wanting you to drive for him?"

"He is not after me," Mike said vehemently, but she couldn't help but remember the way he had run his finger down the side of her neck. Just thinking about it gave her goose bumps. Determinedly she shook the feeling away. "And I have no earthly idea why he wants me to chauffeur him around. So you can just march right out there and tell him to go away. The answer is no. I'm not interested."

"You'll have to tell him then," Vicki said, still grinning. "I've already tried, and he won't listen to me."

Mike was silent for a moment. "Oh, all right," she said at last, tossing her pencil down on the littered desk. "Let him in. I'll tell him no myself." Her green eyes narrowed as she savored the prospect, and she missed the satisfied smile on Vicki's face as the secretary opened the door to invite Devlin Wingate into the tiny inner office of Unicorn Limousine Service.

Saying no to the arrogant Mr. Devlin Wingate would be a distinct pleasure, Mike thought. As Vicki said, it probably wasn't something that happened to him very often. She sat up a little straighter in her chair and folded her hands over the papers on her desk, trying to look as businesslike and formidable as possible. Maybe

Vicki couldn't say no, but *she'd* have him out of here in two seconds flat. She looked up expectantly as he stepped into her office.

The first thing she noticed was his clothes. He was dressed much as he had been when she had picked him up at the airport, except that today his three-piece suit was charcoal gray, two shades darker than his eyes, instead of navy. And his shirt, instead of being crisply white, was an equally crisp pale ice pink. His tie was a deep maroon silk patterned with diagonal gray pinstripes, and there was a maroon silk hankie peeking out of his breast pocket. He still looked very European and, as Vicki had said, very elegant.

The second thing she noticed was the gleam in his eyes. It was curiously appealing, curiously inviting, curiously disturbing. Mike tried very hard to ignore it.

"Mr. Wingate," she greeted him coolly, barely inclining her head in acknowledgement. "What a pleasure to see you again," she said, her husky voice informing him that it wasn't a pleasure at all.

One dark eyebrow sliding upward in amusement as he returned her greeting, Devlin stood just inside the doorway for a moment. "I'm sure it is," he drawled.

He brushed past Vicki with barely a glance in the shapely secretary's direction and, without waiting for an invitation, neatly folded his long, lean length into the chair in front of Mike's desk.

How very typical, Mike reflected, watching him steadily, calmly, over her folded hands. As arrogant as Lucifer—*and twice as handsome,* came the unbidden thought.

Silently Devlin returned her scrutiny. His eyes traveled from the cap of ginger curls that tumbled over her forehead and neck, across her freckled face and generous mouth, down the line of her throat, to linger consideringly on the soft rise and fall of her breasts under the faded blue denim shirt she wore. It was obvious that she wasn't wearing a bra.

"It's a pleasure to see you again, too," he said and then grinned engagingly. "And, unlike you, I mean it. You're a very lovely woman."

Mike's mouth dropped open. No one, not in all her twenty-four years, had ever called her lovely. She had heard herself described as wholesome, outdoorsy, sometimes—God forbid—even as cute, but never lovely! The man must be crazier than she'd first thought.

"Now," he continued before she could gather her wits, "what's this nonsense about you refusing to drive for me?"

"It's not nonsense," Mike snapped, refocusing her attention on the matter at hand. The soundness of his mind, she decided, was not her concern. "It's a fact. I own Unicorn Limousine Service; I'm not one of the drivers."

"You picked me up at the airport the other day," he reminded her.

"As I'm sure my secretary told you, that was due to an unavoidable emergency. I was only filling in."

"So?" His eyebrow slid up again, giving him a lordly air. Mike struggled not to be attracted by it. "Consider this an emergency, too. I need a driver."

"I'm sure you do," Mike agreed smoothly. "And I have several excellent drivers available." She picked up her previously discarded pencil, signaling that their discussion was at an end. "If you'll check with Vicki on your way out, she'll be happy to arrange for one of them to drive you."

"I don't want one of your drivers," he said firmly. "I want you."

Mike heard the implied command in his words, and her temper began to slip. "Well, that's just too bad, isn't it? Because you're not going to get me," she said a little heatedly. Deliberately she bent her head over the papers on her desk, dismissing him.

There was a second or two of tense silence as Mike waited for what her visitor would do next. Would he try to argue with her some more, or would he accept defeat gracefully? He rose from his chair then, as if preparing to leave, and Mike couldn't help the triumphant little smile that curved her lips. Saying no was easy, she thought, if you knew how.

But she was congratulating herself too early, because, instead of heading for the door, Devlin leaned across the desk, his palms flat on its polished surface as he confronted her.

"Wanna bet?" he said very softly.

Mike's head shot up, startled by the challenge in his voice. His eyes were only inches away from hers, so close that she could see tiny twin images of herself reflected in the dark pupils.

"'Bet'?" she echoed vaguely, unconsciously pressing back into her chair. "I don't understand."

No, she didn't understand, he thought. But that was all right because he didn't really understand what was happening, either. He didn't usually chase after women this way, especially when the woman in question had made her disinterest in him so clear. It wasn't his style at all. *Usually* he waited for the women to come to him or, at least, expected them to meet him halfway. But this was different. The way this particular woman affected him was not like the way any other woman had ever affected him.

It wasn't as if the feelings that were racing through him now weren't familiar. He'd felt the same kind of sexual interest in many women, many times before, but it had never come upon him as quickly as it had the other day. What was even more surprising was the realization that his interest had escalated so quickly—and so fiercely—into desire.

He knew that it would be best for all concerned if he would just do as she suggested and accept one of her drivers. But he didn't want one of her drivers: he wanted her. And he wanted her, he realized with something like shock, in the most primitive way possible—naked, in bed, and as much on fire for him as he was for her. He had a sudden image of her spread out beneath him against the pale blue sheets on his bed, her sleek, freckled body glowing like a flame, burning his hands when he touched her.

It didn't even occur to him in that charged moment that getting Mike behind the wheel of a car was a long way from getting her into his bed. But that didn't matter, either. Devlin was a man who worked best when he trusted his instincts, and his instincts were telling him that this was the first step to getting what he wanted.

"I'll pay you double your usual fee," he said, still holding her gaze.

"Double my usual...?" Mike's voice trailed off, and she blinked once, trying to break his hold on her, but she couldn't seem to tear her eyes away from the intensity of his. Her mouth was pursed softly, still formed around the last word.

It took all the control Devlin had to keep from reaching for her. Instinctively he knew that to touch her now, to take her by the shoulders and kiss her until they were both breathless, would only scare her off and make her all the more determined not to drive for him.

"Triple the amount," he said, his voice husky with the effort to control his desire.

"Triple!" Mike echoed. She managed then to look away from him as the amount of money he was offering finally penetrated her fogged brain. Triple her usual amount was more than a hundred-fifty dollars an hour if he wanted the same custom stretch limo that she had used to pick him up at the airport. Add the automatic twenty percent gratuity... and the three hour minimum charge and ... He was crazy! He had to be!

She glanced down at the papers on her desk, a tiny frown furrowing her smooth forehead. He was offering a lot of money—money that would come in handy in paying off that loan ahead of time—but she couldn't help wondering *why* he was willing to pay so much for her to be his chauffeur.

You know why, she told herself. *You're not that naive.*

No, she wasn't that naive. She could sense his sexual interest in her. What she didn't understand was why it was directed at her. She just wasn't the type of woman who incited men to lust. Especially not men like Devlin Wingate. Abruptly she shoved her chair back and stood up. She couldn't think with him bent over her like that. Hell, she thought, she could barely even think with him in the same room!

Devlin straightened at the same time and backed away from the desk, deliberately putting space between himself and this woman who seemed totally unaware of his urgent and incredible desire to tear her clothes off. What a pleasure it would be, he thought, to count and kiss every freckle on her body.

"Now let me get this straight," she began. She kept her glance directed downward, her fingers absently shifting through the papers on the desk, so that she missed the hungry way his eyes were roving over her body. Her jeans were snug fitting, faded to white at the seams from years of wear, and they followed the gentle curve of her hips like a caress, molding the length of her firm, slender thighs with disturbing thoroughness. "You're offering me triple my usual hourly fee to be your driver." She looked up. "Is that right?"

"That's right." Devlin nodded, his eyes snapping back to her face as he spoke. And it was the truth, he told himself: his offer of payment was only in exchange for her being his driver.

"Just for being your driver?" she said, her eyes still questioning him across the width of the desk. "Nothing else?"

"Nothing—" Devlin began and then stopped. Maybe, he thought, she *was* aware of his interest in her. Her words certainly implied that she had sensed something, didn't they? *Of course she senses something, you jackass,* he said to himself. Why else would she want to be sure that driving was all he had in mind?

Mike was still looking at him expectantly, her eyes wide as she waited for him to complete his sentence, but he just stood there, looking back at her with that...that almost fanatical gleam in his eyes.

Was he teasing her, Mike wondered, misreading his expression. Was he leading her down some twisted path of his own in order to make fun of her? True, he didn't exactly look like he was teasing, she thought, but growing up with two older brothers who had teased her unmercifully had made her wary.

What was he up to?

"Just driving?" she said again. "That's all?"

"That's all," he repeated after her. A smile curved his lips for a moment. "Unless you'd like something more?" he said, his head tilted sideways.

"Unless I—" Mike bit the words off furiously. Damn! He *had* been making fun of her, and she'd walked right into it, like a lamb to the slaughter. Unless . . . unless she'd misunderstood what he'd said. But, no, she thought in the next instant. What else could he have meant besides some nasty little sexual innuendo? Still, she hesitated. She never had been any good at these silly

little male-female games. She had never played them—
had never been given the opportunity to play them—
and she didn't understand the rules.

So, regardless of what he did or didn't mean, she decided, regardless of the money he was offering, she'd
be better off, *safer*, to say no. She opened her mouth to
tell him just that.

Devlin, realizing that he had made a tactical error,
hurried to mend it. "Scared?" he challenged softly.

"'Scared'!" Mike repeated scathingly, completely
forgetting the negation that had been hovering on her
lips. Daring Mike had always had the same effect as
waving a red cape in front of a bull; she charged first
and thought about it later. "Of what?" Her eyes raked
him contemptuously from the top of his elegant black
head to the toes of his brilliantly polished shoes. *"You?"*
she said scornfully.

Devlin gave her a careless little nod, for all the world
like royalty acknowledging the applause of the masses,
and the expression on his face was definitely smug.
There was no other word for it.

What an ego the man has, she thought, her eyes narrowing dangerously. *Besides being rude and arrogant,
he thinks he's irresistible, too*. Somebody ought to teach
him a lesson in humility. Somebody ought to . . .

Mike struggled valiantly to control her temper,
knowing that if she said anything right now, she would
regret it later. But she couldn't control the look in her
eyes. They blazed at Devlin, shooting tiny sparks of
green fire aimed right at his smug, handsome face.

Oh, yes, Devlin thought then, completely entranced by the emotions that flickered across her freckled face: incredulity, temper, challenge. He wanted her more than ever and knew that if he was going to get her he had to do something quick, before the "No" that he could still see in her eyes made it past her lips. He grinned, a patronizing, challenging, thoroughly male grin. "Or maybe you don't trust yourself to be alone with me?" he said, goading her.

That did it!

He thought she didn't trust herself to be alone with him, did he? Of all the conceited, arrogant—"You've got a deal, Mr. Wingate," Mike said furiously, unable to hold on to her temper any longer. She rounded the desk like a whirlwind, brushing past the grinning Devlin to fling open the connecting door to Vicki's office. "Fill in the paperwork for Mr. Wingate," she said to her startled secretary. "At *triple* the regular fee. I'm going to change." She treated the outer door to the same rough handling, slamming it shut behind her as she headed for the locker room.

3

MIKE'S TEMPER sustained her through the ten minutes it took to change into her chauffeur's uniform. And it sustained her through the fifteen minutes it took to go through her routine predrive check of the limousine's amenities. Propelled by furious efficiency, she filled the ice bucket and the coffee thermos, checked the dispensers for liquor and tissues, made sure that the interior of the car was delicately scented with the aerosol fragrance of fresh flowers, and wiped off any unsightly fingerprints that might possibly have been left by the last occupant of the back seat.

But nothing could sustain her when it was time to drive the silver stretch Cadillac out of the parking garage and around to the office door to pick up her passenger.

He was standing at the front entrance, one shoulder propped against the painted doorframe, his head tilted and eyes crinkled against the fierce summer sun as he watched the big silver car glide toward him. His arms were casually folded across his chest, and his left leg was slightly bent and crossed over his right so that the toe of his shiny black shoe rested against the ground.

Try as she might, Mike couldn't help but notice how the pale pink of his starched shirt turned his tan to gleaming gold, and how the sun brought out the blue highlights in his glossy black hair. A soft wave of that hair dipped over his forehead, as if by accident, giving an appealing hint of rakishness to what otherwise would have been a flawless appearance.

He looked, Mike admitted unwillingly, just the way she had imagined every hero in every Regency romance she had ever read. Absolutely beautiful; the epitome of classic masculine elegance; Lord Byron in a three-piece suit.

But, she reminded herself as she felt her temper melting away, he *acted* just like every Regency hero she had ever read about, too. He was arrogant, used to getting his own way, demanding her services as if she were a...an impoverished governess whom he had his eye on. And, like a silly, spineless governess in a bad novel, she had actually given in to his demand.

"You and your stupid temper," she muttered to herself as she pulled the car to a smooth stop.

She didn't want to drive for this man. Hell, she didn't want to drive for anyone. She was the owner of Unicorn Limousines, not a driver. At least, she amended, not anymore. Not unless there was an emergency like the other day. Or unless one of her old reliable customers asked especially for her. Well, Devlin Wingate wasn't an old customer, but he *had* asked for her. Demanded her, she reminded herself. And he *was* paying triple the regular price. Besides, a deal was a deal.

And I'll be damned if I'll give him the satisfaction of backing out now, she thought as she slid out of the car and moved to open the passenger door. Determined to treat the disturbing Mr. Devlin Wingate as if he were just another customer, Mike opened the rear door with a little flourish, her free hand crossed in front of her waist, palm up in a presenting gesture as she motioned toward the interior of the car. Her eyes were downcast, focused on the plush back seat, as she subtly directed him in.

"Can't I sit in the front with you?" Devlin asked.

"With me?" Mike's eyes flew up for a moment, meeting the sparkling gleam in his, then dropped instantly.

He was teasing her again, and she hated to be teased. It embarrassed her. She didn't know how to respond to it, except with a show of temper—and that response had already gotten her into enough trouble with this man.

"No, Mr. Wingate, I'm afraid you can't," she replied, taking refuge in her best professional chauffeur's manner. Whatever her deficiencies on a more intimate level, she could handle men quite easily in a business situation, and she strove now to keep everything businesslike between them. "Regulations, uh, forbid a paying customer to sit in the front." The regulations said nothing of the kind, but it was the first thing that came to her mind that would keep him in the back where he belonged.

"Can't you make an exception?" he coaxed with a beguiling smile. "Just this once?"

Mike fixed him with a stern stare. "Do you want me to risk losing my license?" she asked, trying valiantly to ignore what that devastating smile was doing to her insides.

"No, certainly not." Devlin sighed and climbed into the back seat. Lord, this woman was going to be a hard nut to crack, he thought. It made him want her all the more.

Steeling herself, Mike leaned into the back seat after him, one gloved hand braced against the front edge of the doorframe. "This is the bar," she said, determined to do the thing right this time. "Scotch, bourbon, vodka, soda, tonic and plain water." She pointed to each button as she spoke, deliberately keeping her face turned away from the man who was watching her every move with fascinated attention. "They dispense approximately one jigger each time you press the…" Her voice trailed off as she sensed him move forward on the seat as if to better see what she was showing him. Mike gulped. "The, uh, button," she finished, barely able to remember what it was she had been saying.

"It's a little early in the day to begin drinking, don't you think?" he said, his voice coming from somewhere near her right ear. He was so close she could feel the warmth of his breath on her cheek as he spoke.

Carefully Mike inched away and went on, forcing herself to be crisply professional. "There's hot coffee in the thermos," she offered, her eyes stubbornly averted from his as she pointed it out. "Sweetener and powdered creamer here. Glasses and cups are in here." She opened and closed a small door, offering him a glimpse of crystal bar glasses and china cups, each nestled in separate padded compartments. "Ice bucket here. And—*Mr. Wingate, please!*"

She jumped back as he touched her shoulder and thumped her head on the upholstered roof of the car in her haste to avoid him. Her eyes shifted warily to his as her hand went to the back of her head to rub the spot she had whacked. He was looking at her with that . . . that predatory gleam in his eyes again.

Mike's careful professional facade crumbled in the face of that look. Her hand dropped from the back of her head. Her eyes narrowed. "I don't care what you're paying—I do *not* come with the price of the limousine!"

"Did I say you did?" Devlin said blandly, sinking back into the plush upholstery of the seat. He crossed his arms over his chest again, his head tilted to the side as he considered her.

"No, but you're . . . you . . ." He did what? She tried to clarify the situation. Put his hand on her shoulder? Well, that wasn't exactly an overt sexual advance, was it? No, of course not. And yet, somehow, it was. The look in those gray eyes, that teasing, seductive, thoroughly masculine, subtly challenging look, made it one.

"Please keep your hands to yourself from now on," she said primly, staunchly ignoring the color that was creeping up from under the collar of her uniform.

"I'm sorry," Devlin said, not looking the least bit sorry. Not if that lazy smile was anything to go by. "I just wondered what the material of your uniform was made of. You look awfully, er—" his smile became a teasing grin as he hesitated over the word "—warm."

Warm! Hell, yes, she was warm. She felt like she was about to melt—from the inside out.

"Yes...well," she stammered, looking anywhere but at Devlin, "I guess I am a bit warm. But the sun's pretty fierce today," she offered, knowing that the sun had very little to do with the heated flush of her skin. "It always is, this time of year," she added, as if he didn't already know that. "But my uniform...all my chauffeurs' uniforms are made with the Texas climate in mind. It's very lightweight. Very comfortable. It—"

"Very sexy, too."

Mike flashed him a quick sideways look, searching for the hidden meaning behind his words. He meant it, she realized, her eyes widening incredulously. He actually did think the uniform was sexy. "Well, uh..." She had no idea how to respond to a compliment about her appearance, even so mild a one as that. "Well, I..." Her shoulders lifted in a little shrug. "Thank you," she said finally, not knowing what else to say. Then she made a firm motion toward the control panel, determined to get this conversation back on a business footing.

As if, she thought derisively, *it had ever been there to begin with.*

"These are the controls for the television," she said quickly, pointing them out. "The VCR. Radio. Telephone. Air-conditioning. Sunroof. Reading lights." She straightened purposefully. "Any questions?"

Devlin shook his head. "Not any that I care to ask right now." His slow smile was a definite promise of things to come. "Maybe later."

"Well, that's, uh... That's fine," Mike managed. She slammed the rear door shut and reached blindly for the handle on the front door of the car.

Dummy! she thought, mentally kicking herself as she slid into the driver's seat. *You sounded like some half-witted idiot. Hell, you are a half-witted idiot. Stumbling all over yourself like some dopey tongue-tied teenager just because some big-headed arrogant egotistical*—Mike's thoughts floundered for a moment as she groped for the proper word—*playboy,* she decided with a little nod of her head, *gives you one measly little compliment.*

Savagely she twisted the key in the ignition, revving the engine to life, then glanced into the rearview mirror. "Where to, Mr. Wingate?" she asked crisply, determined once and for all to keep this relationship on a strictly business footing.

"Take LBJ to the Dallas Parkway, then head north. I'll tell you when to stop," he said, smiling into her eyes.

Mike's glance skittered away from the mirror, unable to hold his, and she headed the big silver car out of the driveway and onto the street. Turning north when she reached the parkway, she drove sedately past a jungle of tall spindly-looking construction cranes and half-finished high-rise buildings that littered the street on both sides, attesting to the rapid growth of the area. Adding to the confusion of the midmorning traffic were busy road crews and city-erected barricades that redirected the line of cars around long sections of broken asphalt. The street was being widened to accommodate the increased traffic that the surge of new build-

ings would bring to an already congested stretch of
road.

It was, from a driver's point of view, a complete
mess: gaping potholes ready to disable the unwary,
bulldozers backing up, mounds of gravel and dirt,
lengths of concrete sewer pipe lining the road in apparently random arrangements, sudden stops and unexpected lane changes by inattentive or inexperienced
fellow drivers. It took all of Mike's considerable ex-
pertise to maneuver the big stretch Caddy smoothly
through and around all the obstacles in its path.

It also required all her attention, and Mike gave it
eagerly, thankful to have an excuse not to talk to her
disturbing passenger. Knowing that he was sitting behind her, just waiting to catch her eye in the rearview
mirror, was bad enough.

"Take a left after you get through the light," Devlin
instructed quietly, fully aware of the concentration required for Mike to safely do her job. "That next construction site, right there." Mike caught a blur of
movement in the rearview mirror as he motioned with
one hand. "Just pull up next to that trailer."

Nodding to indicate that she had heard him, Mike
turned smoothly off the road. Bits of gravel crunched
under the tires as she left the asphalt, and a cloud of dust
rose up from the ground beneath the car, coating its
shining surface with a thin film of some of Dallas's most
expensive real estate. She turned off the ignition, waited
a few seconds for the dust to settle and then slid out of
the car, hurrying to open the passenger door before
Devlin could move to do it himself.

"Sir," she said smartly, automatically extending her hand to help him from the plush back seat, just as she would with any other passenger. It was a mistake. His clasp was firm and warm, even through the fabric of her gray gloves, and it lasted just a moment too long for mere civility. Mike felt a sudden burst of warmth go tingling up her arm, as if she had put her finger into a light socket. Devlin grinned and gave her a flirtatious wink, as if to say he knew exactly what she was feeling.

Mike gasped indignantly and started to snatch her hand back, but it was unnecessary. Devlin had already let her go. Turning away, he extended his hand to the man in leather work boots and a hard hat who came striding up to greet him.

"Dickson." He clasped the other man's hand in a firm grasp, his countenance suddenly all business. "How're things going?"

"Real fine, Mr. Wingate. Real fine," the man answered, enthusiastically pumping Devlin's arm. "Your daddy's office called my girl this morning. Said you'd—" the whine of a drill suddenly pierced the air, and he automatically raised his voice to compensate for it "—be coming to look us over." He made a sweeping gesture with the roll of papers in his left hand, indicating the construction site behind him. "There's a lot to see," he shouted. "Work's been going like a house afire."

"Let's see it then," Devlin shouted back, turning toward the dusty green-and-white trailer. "Starting with the office. I want to check some figures that you sent down from..." His voice was drowned out by the buzz of men and equipment as he moved away from the car.

Mike stood where she was for a moment more, her left hand still on the door handle as she watched Devlin disappear into the trailer with the jovial Dickson, her right hand cradled against her waist. She dropped it guiltily, looking around to see if anyone had noticed the ridiculous way she had been holding it, like a groupie who'd had her hand touched by Bruce Springsteen and was never going to wash it again. No one was paying the least bit of attention to her.

Thank goodness, she thought, slamming the rear door with a bang. *I've made a fool of myself enough for one day.*

Sighing, she stripped off her gloves and reached into the front seat to rummage around in her voluminous chauffeur's carryall. In it she carried all the tools of her trade—and then some. Assorted screwdrivers and wrenches, paper towels, plastic trash bags, flares, a flashlight, a small fire extinguisher, a tire gauge, battery cables, gum, mints, aspirin, sewing and shoe-shine kits, Band-Aids, antacids, a siphon hose... anything and everything she might possibly need during the course of a day as a chauffeur. Finding what she wanted, she straightened and, closing the front door with the thrust of her hip, began to clean the car windows with a spray bottle of window cleaner and a wad of paper towels. Dust had settled everywhere.

With all the construction going on, the car would probably be coated again almost as soon as she cleaned it off, but she had nothing better to do. Devlin Wingate hadn't seen fit to tell her how long they might be here, and she didn't want to stand around doing nothing while she waited for him. Besides, her father had always said that idle hands made for idle thoughts. And Mike's thoughts were idle enough as it was.

She looked down at the hand Devlin had held, watching as it smoothed over the surface of the glass in steady circular motions. Funny how the simple touch of another hand—the hard male hand of an almost-stranger—had made hers tingle like that, sending little ripples of sensation running up and down her arm. She hadn't felt anything remotely like it in a long time. Not since she was fourteen and suffering from a bad case of puppy love for her oldest brother's best friend.

Of course, the love had been unrequited; poor Carl hadn't had a clue that he had been cast as the hero of her teenage daydreams, and he would have been horrified if he had known. Good ol' Mike, freckle-faced shortstop on the boys' baseball team, scourge of the neighborhood skating rink, the best mechanic in Shop and the tallest, skinniest girl in ninth grade, wasn't the stuff of which romantic dreams were made. Then—or now.

So why did Devlin Wingate look at her like he was a starving man, and she was the Blue Plate Special?

Mike stared down into the face reflected in the windshield, trying to see what could possibly have attracted him. She wasn't beautiful, not even pretty really when compared to the ebony-haired beauty who had been waiting for Devlin at his condo. In fact, she hadn't changed all that much from what she had been at fourteen. Still skinny. Still freckle-faced. Still "good ol' Mike."

Certainly nothing there to seriously attract a man like Devlin Wingate, she decided, pausing to dab the sleeve of her jacket lightly against her damp forehead. No sophistication, no beauty, no sex appeal. Still, he had called her "a lovely woman." He thought her uniform was sexy. And there was the way he looked at her. No man had ever looked at her in quite that way before. It must mean *something*.

Mike met her own eyes in the darkened windshield. Oh, it meant something all right, she thought. It meant that either the man was just amusing himself by playing with her—or he was seriously crazy.

"And you are even crazier for even thinking about it," she said to herself. "So stop it," she ordered her reflection. "Now."

She made one last swipe at the window with her wad of paper towels, then moved around to the front of the car. Dropping to her haunches, she began wiping down the chrome bumper and grill, one ear cocked for the sound of the trailer door opening. At the first creak of the metal door whining against its hinges, she sprang up from her half crouch. Seeing who it was, she placed her cleaning implements on the hood and hurried around to the passenger door. Opening it, she stood at attention with her hand on the handle as Devlin came toward her.

This time, she told herself firmly, watching him out of the corner of her eye, this time she would be strictly professional, strictly business, no matter what he said or did.

And then he did the unexpected again. Pausing just short of entering the limousine, he tossed his briefcase inside so that it bounced lightly on the plush upholstered seat. Then, instead of climbing in after it, he casually removed his elegant gray jacket and tossed that onto the back seat, too. Next came his trim-fitting vest.

Mike's eyes widened, her fingers tightening on the door handle as she watched him remove the vest. His shoulders were broad, his back lean, with long smooth muscles that curved and flexed as he removed the vest, pulling at the fabric of his custom-fitted shirt. It was the kind of back she would have expected to see under the dirt-smeared shirt of a rodeo cowboy, like her oldest brother Harlan. The kind of back that should have a streak of sweat running down the middle of it. The kind of back . . . He turned toward her then, and Mike's eyes widened even more. He was just as impressive from this angle.

"Here, hold these."

"What?" Mike said vacantly, making no move to take what he held out to her. She simply stood there, staring at the broad expanse of his chest and feeling very much as if she had been deliberately misled by the way his tailor-made jacket had concealed the rangy, rugged masculinity of his build. Wasn't there a law against false advertising?

"These." Devlin picked up her hand and dropped something small and cool into her palm. He curled her fingers closed. "Keep them for me until I get back."

"Get back?" Mike slowly lifted her eyes to his. "Are you going somewhere?"

Devlin grinned and squeezed her hand lightly. "Not if you don't want me to, I won't," he said, teasing her again.

Mike snatched her hand away, her fingers still curled around the cuff links. "I don't want you, period!" she said, reacting to the teasing tone without stopping to consider her words. If she had stopped to think, she'd have realized how revealing the statement was. It showed him exactly where her mind had been for the past twenty minutes.

"You just think you don't." Devlin's voice was complacent. Knowing. Rich with a sense of simple masculine conceit.

"I just think I . . . ?" Words failed her.

"But that's okay," he added when she continued to stand there with her mouth open. "Because you will."

"I will . . . ?"

"Yes, you will." His eyes, crinkled up against sunlight and amusement, were totally confident. As far as he was concerned, he was stating the simple, unequivocal truth. She wanted him as much as he wanted her. She just didn't know it yet—but she would. Yes, she most definitely would, he thought with satisfaction. Soon.

"I will . . . ?" Mike moved her mouth like a fish gasping for air. The man's ego was truly amazing! "I . . . Oh! I'll show you *I will*," she began furiously, completely forgetting her vow to treat him like any other paying customer. She took a half step forward, her chin tilted pugnaciously, the hand clutching the cuff links lifted slightly, as if she meant to throw them. The shards of gold in her eyes turned lethal as she stared up at him.

Oh, those eyes, he thought, meeting her angry glare with a suddenly smoldering look. She could bring a man to his knees with her eyes alone. He lifted his hands to her shoulders and gripped them lightly. "Yes," he breathed softly, hardly aware of what he was saying. "Oh, yes. Show me how you will."

Mike stilled, her gaze softening abruptly as it tangled with the smoke of his, her quick anger forgotten in a rush of other, more powerful emotions. Her chin remained tilted but no longer belligerent. Her half-raised fist was motionless between them. She waited for what he would do next, as still and helpless as a mouse waiting for the strike of a hungry snake. Devlin lowered his head.

Just then the trailer door was thrown back on its hinges, banging loudly against the metal siding of the trailer. "Got that hard hat for you, Mr. Wingate," Dickson's voice boomed. His work boots crunched on the gravel as he stepped off the single concrete step in front of the trailer door.

Mike stiffened under Devlin's hands, her eyes widening with a sudden awareness of what had almost happened. What she had almost *let* happen. She drew back, her clenched hand touching Devlin's chest in protest. "No," she whispered, the word more a movement of her lips than a sound.

For just a moment she thought he might resist, might kiss her, anyway, but then he sighed and dropped his hands from her shoulders as he lifted his head, silently accepting her refusal. Mike was appalled at the wave of disappointment that washed over her.

"You're right," he murmured. "Now isn't the time."

"The time will be never," Mike managed shakily, a saving spark of temper piercing her disappointment.

Devlin shook his head, his eyes steady on hers. "Later," he corrected her. There was absolute conviction in his voice. Then, before Mike could think of a suitably scathing retort, he turned away, one hand reaching for the yellow hard hat that Dickson held out to him.

"The men are working on the fourteenth floor right now," Dickson said as Devlin adjusted the hat on his head. "I expect to be . . ." His voice was overwhelmed by the sounds of construction and traffic as the two men moved across the ravaged ground toward the half-finished office building. Devlin nodded, absently rolling up the sleeves of his pale pink shirt as he matched steps with the other man. They disappeared into the metal cage that rested at the base of the structure.

Mike stood where she was, her gaze following the elevator's clanging ascent up the side of the building, her hand still curled around the tiny silver cuff links in her palm. Her lips were slightly parted, tingling, as if he had actually touched them with his.

Later.

The word echoed in her head, his tone of utter conviction coming through loud and clear. He hadn't been teasing her, she realized. He had been dead serious. And if he wasn't teasing, then he was surely crazy. She thought again of the smoldering look that had been in his eyes, that smoldering, smoky, seductive look. *For her.*

Yes, the man was definitely crazy.

4

MIKE BURST THROUGH the office door, closing it behind her with a quick, furious flick of her wrist. A large silver-framed picture of a 1928 Stutz Bearcat bounced against the wall as the door slammed shut, trembling precariously on its single hook. Mike didn't even notice it.

"That man is the most egotistical, most arrogant—" She threw her gray chauffeur's cap against the wall. Two days of driving for Devlin Wingate had taken their toll on her. "Most *infuriating* man I have ever met."

"What man is that?" Vicki asked absently, glancing up from the open schedule book on her desk.

Mike stared at her, her freckled face screwed up in a threatening glare.

"Oh, *that* man," Vicki said, hiding a smile. She needn't have bothered. Mike wasn't looking at her, not really. All her attention was focused inward, feeding on her temper and the something else that she hadn't yet admitted to herself.

"Yes, *that* man." Mike flung herself into one of the chairs in front of Vicki's desk and ran her hands through her flattened ginger hair, automatically fluffing it. "You wouldn't believe what he did! What he said! I can't— He's the most—" Words failed her. She shifted in her chair, throwing one long leg over the arm, and scowled at the toe of her gray pump. "Infuriating!"

"You said that already," Vicki reminded her.

"Well, he is, dammit!"

"Yes, I know," Vicki said soothingly. She closed the schedule book and folded her hands on top of it. "Tell Vicki all about it," she invited. "What did the nasty infuriating man do this time?"

Mike flashed her a quick look, ready to pounce, and then grinned sheepishly when she saw the expression on her secretary's face. "God, I sound like a real idiot, don't I?"

Vicki grinned back. "You said it—I didn't."

Mike went back to scowling at her shoe. "It's just that he really gets to me."

"It's about time someone did."

"He actually had the nerve to ask me..." She paused as Vicki's words registered. Lifting her eyes from the contemplation of her shoe, Mike stared at her secretary. "What did you say?"

"I said 'It's about time someone did.'"

"Did what?"

"Got to you."

"Got to me?" Comprehension dawned. The green eyes widened innocently. "Oh, come on, Vicki," she scoffed. "I didn't mean like *that*."

Vicki gave her a wry, knowing look. "Didn't you?"

"No! Of course not." She jumped to her feet and took a quick turn around the small office. "It's just that he's so damn arrogant. That's what gets to me. He's obviously had everything handed to him on a silver platter.

I mean, for two days I've had to watch people falling all over themselves to get him what he wanted before he even had a chance to ask for it! 'Yes, Mr. Wingate. No, Mr. Wingate. Shall I cut off my right arm, Mr. Wingate?'" she mimicked disgustedly, still pacing. "He thinks he can have anything he wants, anytime he wants it." She came to a stop in front of her secretary's desk. "His attitude bugs me, that's all."

"Uh-huh."

"Well, it does!"

"Uh-huh," Vicki said again. "I think the lady doth protest too much."

"And just what do you mean by that?" Mike asked.

"You know very well what I mean by that," Vicki said. "It's not just his so-called arrogant attitude that's got you riled up, it's him, the man himself. *He's* what gets to you," she guessed shrewdly. "I'm right, aren't I?" she prodded when Mike didn't answer.

Mike shrugged. Unwilling to admit that Vicki spoke the truth, she stood and stared at the floor, one hand fiddling with the papers in Vicki's In basket.

"I'm right," Vicki said with conviction. "The thing is, what are you going to do about it?"

Mike shrugged again. "Nothing." She lifted her eyes to her secretary's. "Because there's nothing to do anything about," she added almost defiantly, as if daring Vicki to dispute it.

"Nothing? Are you crazy? You've got a man like Devlin Wingate running after you with his tongue hanging out, and you're going to do *nothing*?" She reached across the desk and took Mike's wrist in her slender fingers.

"What are you doing?"

"Checking your pulse," Vicki said tartly. "You must have died without anybody noticing it."

Mike jerked her hand away and flopped back into the burgundy chair. "Very funny."

"No, it's not funny." Vicki's soft voice was suddenly serious. "A handsome, sexy man—an honest-to-God Texas millionaire, no less!—expresses a perfectly normal interest in you, and what do you do?" She flung up her hands in disgust. "You get mad about it."

"How do you know he's a millionaire?" Mike challenged sulkily, hoping to change the subject. "Just because he acts like he's stinking rich." She shrugged.

"Honey, he *is* stinking rich. I've been doing a little discreet investigating," Vicki told her. "The Wingates are old money." She rolled her eyes expressively. "Very old money. They've been here since before Texas was a republic and are into everything. And I mean *everything*. Oil, of course—"

"Of course." Mike's voice dripped sarcasm.

"Office buildings, shopping malls, hotels, a shipping line, construction, electronics. You name it, they seem to be involved in it. And—" she produced this last bit of information as if it were accompanied by a trumpet flourish "—Devlin Wingate is an only son."

"And on the basis of that, I suppose you think I should run after him with *my* tongue hanging out."

"It'd be a step in the right direction."

Mike shook her head stubbornly. "He's not my type," she lied.

Vicki snorted. "That man is every woman's type."

"Fine." Mike slumped even farther down in the chair and glared across the desk. "You run after him."

Vicki gave a silvery little laugh. "Believe me, if I thought it would do any good, I would. But I already gave it my best shot." She sighed and shook back the tangle of blond hair that had fallen over one eye. "He isn't the least bit interested in me. Like I said—" she grinned and pointed a pink-tipped finger at Mike "—it's you he wants."

"But why?" Mike wailed softly, tacitly admitting the truth of Vicki's statement, although she honestly didn't understand why it should be so. She waved a hand down the length of her long, lean body, sprawled in the office chair. "What have I got that a man like Devlin Wingate could possibly want?"

Compassion and anger filled Vicki's blue eyes. "Just because that bozo-brain cowboy you thought you were in love with didn't know a real woman when he had one, doesn't mean every other man in the world is deaf, dumb and blind, too."

Mike stiffened in her seat. "This hasn't got anything to do with Dan," she objected. It was partially true. Mostly true. What had happened between her and Dan—or rather, what hadn't happened—wasn't the reason she avoided relationships with men. It had only been the final straw.

"Oh, doesn't it?" Vicki pressed on. "Isn't Dan the reason you haven't dated anybody for the past four years?"

"I date."

"Uh-huh. When was the last time?"

Mike thought for a moment. "Arnie Brubaker."

"Lunch with your bank's loan officer doesn't count. Who else?"

"Uh, Steve Gillis."

"He's your cousin. And three years younger than you." Vicki dismissed him with a wave of her hand. "Who else?"

Mike thought again, her freckled face screwed up in concentration. She couldn't remember anyone else. "I'm too busy building up the business to think about dating right now," she said. "What with using up most of my cash reserves to buy out Billy Ray and that loan for the Silver Wraith hanging over my head..." She shrugged. "It takes all my time just to hustle up more customers."

Vicki looked at her, her mouth pursed in an expression of disbelief and good-natured disgust.

"Well, I didn't exactly date a lot before Dan either, so what difference does it make? Besides, men aren't everything, you know."

"They aren't nothing, either," Vicki countered.

"To me they are," Mike insisted stubbornly, her chin up.

"Oh, really?" Vicki's penciled blond eyebrows rose. "Is that why you're in such a tizzy? Because Devlin Wingate's a nothing?"

"He hasn't got me in a tizzy!"

"Oh, right. Uh-huh. You're just stomping and swearing and throwing things—" with a nod of her head she indicated the chauffeur's cap on the floor "—because it's Thursday, right? And you always throw things on Thursdays."

"Okay, okay!" Mike came upright in the chair. "So I'm a little upset. So what? You'd be upset, too, if some arrogant overbearing playboy acted like you should be honored to go out with him. I can't believe—"

"Wait a minute." Vicki held up a slim hand. "Wait just one minute. Is that what this tantrum is all about? Devlin Wingate asked you to go out with him? On a date?"

"Yes, of course, on a date," Mike said huffily. "Where else would he—"

But Vicki wasn't listening. "Well, I'll be damned. He doesn't waste much time, does he?" she said admiringly. "Well, when are you going? Where are you going? Tell me all the juicy details."

"I'm not."

"You're not?" There was a second of stunned silence. "You mean you said no?"

Mike nodded, her chin set at a stubborn angle.

"You actually said no to that gorgeous, sexy, *rich* man?" Vicki shook her head sadly, unbelievingly. "That's it. That proves it. You're definitely certifiable."

"I am not," Mike defended herself. "Just because you'll go out with anyone who asks you doesn't mean that I'm abnormal. Besides," she added, using the same argument she had given Devlin when he had asked her out, "I don't allow my drivers to date customers. How would it look if I did it? No." She gave a decisive shake of her head, her generous mouth thinned to a firm line. "I don't believe in mixing business with pleasure."

"You don't believe in mixing pleasure with anything."

"That's not true," Mike retorted, stung. "I get a lot of pleasure out of this business. I love it."

"I know you love it, Mike," Vicki said soothingly. "I didn't mean it that way. You know I didn't. But business isn't everything."

There was a loud rap on the door, and without waiting for an answer, somebody pushed it open. "Delivery," said a young man. "Guy out there—" he motioned with his head toward the garage "—said it belonged in here." He sauntered across the room and laid a long florist's box on the desk. "Guess these must be for you, doll," he said, grinning at Vicki from under the brim of his cap. He didn't even seem to notice Mike.

Vicki smiled up at him. "Thank you," she murmured, her lashes fluttering automatically as she reached for her purse.

The young man waved the tip away. "Been taken care of."

"Well, who's it from this time?" Mike asked as the office door closed behind the delivery boy. There was a note of wistful envy in her voice. "Your computer genius or the lawyer?"

"I don't know." Vicki's fingers were busily trying to slide a small envelope out from under the wide yellow ribbon. "Leo is out of town and— Oh, these aren't for me." She held the envelope across the desk. There was a big grin on her face. "They're for you."

"Me?" Mike said incredulously. "Who'd be sending me flowers?"

Vicki wagged the envelope at her. "Open it and see." She made as if to draw her hand back across the desk. "Or shall I open it for you?"

"No!" Mike reached out and snatched the envelope from her secretary's fingers. "I'll open it."

"Well?" Vicki urged when Mike just sat there looking at her name written across the envelope. "Open it. I'm dying to know if I'm right."

Slowly, feeling gauche and self-conscious, Mike inserted the tip of her finger under the flap and lifted it. No one had ever sent her flowers before. Never. She hadn't even received a corsage for the Senior Prom like most girls, because, unlike most girls, she hadn't gone to the Senior Prom. No one had asked her.

Not that she had cared, of course. At least, that's what she'd told herself. She was already a businesswoman by that time, proud owner of her first Cadillac, proprietor of a one-driver, one-car limousine service. She had spent the night of the Senior Prom chauffeuring those other girls and their dates from their chosen restaurants to the high school gymnasium. It still hurt to think about it.

"Well?" Vicki prodded. "Is it him?"

Mike slid the card out of its envelope.

"You're fired," it said in bold black script. "Now will you have dinner with me?"

There was no signature, but Mike didn't need one to know who the card was from. Devlin Wingate had sent her flowers.

"Is it him? Is it?"

"Yes," she said at last, her husky voice low and a little awed. Flowers, she thought again. Devlin Wingate had sent her flowers. She bit down on her bottom lip to still its sudden trembling.

"I knew it!" Vicki crowed triumphantly. She nudged the long florist's box across the desk. "Open them," she ordered.

As if in a trance, Mike dropped the card onto the desk and drew the white oblong carton onto her lap. With fingers that shook slightly she untied the yellow ribbon and lifted the lid. "Oh," she gasped softly. "Oh, how lovely. Roses."

They lay nestled in a bed of dark green ferns, drops of water glistening on their long thornless stems. Not white and not quite cream, they were a warm ivory just barely tinged around the edges with a pale blush of coral. Mike dropped the lid to the floor and lifted the box to bury her face in the delicate scent of her first flowers.

"Now are you going out with him?" Vicki asked.

Mike went very still, her face hidden in the flowers. Would she go out with him now? Should she? Did she dare? "No," she replied, lowering the box to her lap.

"No?" Plainly Vicki couldn't believe her ears. "But he sent you those beautiful flowers."

"I know," Mike said, her eyes still glued to her lap. They *were* beautiful flowers, the most beautiful flowers she had ever seen. Roses. She had always loved roses. How had he known that? She sighed and touched one delicate petal with the tip of her finger. "But just because he sent me flowers doesn't mean I'm obligated to change my mind and go out with him, does it?"

"No, but—"

"But nothing. He...he probably sends flowers at the drop of a hat." She faltered a little as she said it, wishing, just for a moment, that the flowers could have meant as much to him as they did to her. But that was impossible and unrealistic. He was a millionaire playboy who had developed an unaccountable lust for a skinny chauffeur. And he didn't like being told no. The flowers were just a way to get what he wanted. "I'll bet he didn't even write the card," she added, more to remind herself of that fact than Vicki.

"So what? Hardly anybody writes their own cards," Vicki informed her. "Most flowers are ordered over the phone, and you tell the florist what you want it to say." She picked up the card from the desk and studied it for a moment, her lips quirking up in a grin as she read the message. "But he did write this one," she said.

Mike looked up from her flowers. "How would you know?"

"I filled out his paperwork yesterday, remember? This is definitely his handwriting." She turned the envelope over and scanned the florist's address, then extracted a folder from the tidy stack on top of her desk. Flipping it open, she ran one finger over the typewritten lines. "Same street address," she said to herself. She looked up at Mike. "There's a florist in his building."

"So?" Mike's chin was tilted at a stubborn angle. "That just means he probably noticed it on his way to the elevator and decided to give it one more try."

"Maybe. But the fact remains that he did send them."

"Yes," Mike agreed, looking down at the flowers in her lap. Her eyes got a little misty and had a faraway look. "He did, didn't he?"

"So what are you going to do about it?"

Mike lifted her chin again. "Nothing," she said resolutely. "A bunch of flowers, no matter how pretty, aren't going to change my mind. I am *not* going to be entertainment for a playboy like Devlin Wingate."

"You sure?" Vicki laughed. "Sounds to me like it might be fun. Okay, okay," she placated when Mike scowled at her. "You're not going to play with Devlin Wingate. Personally, I think you're crazy. But," she hurried on before Mike could respond, "you do owe him a thank-you for the flowers and an answer to this." She tapped the card against the palm of her hand.

Mike's scowl faded, and her eyes widened. Vicki was right. If she didn't call him, he just might show up at her doorstep, expecting her to have dinner with him. Well why not? she thought, giving in to fantasy for just a moment. What could happen over dinner?

But then she remembered what had happened at the construction site. If she had almost succumbed to his charm at high noon, in the midst of bulldozers and jackhammers, she'd be a goner surrounded by candlelight and soft music. Look what just the flowers had done, making her go all trembly and misty-eyed before she'd even opened the box.

She had to face it, she was a sucker for anything romantic and always had been, no matter how hard she tried to pretend otherwise. Her favorite songs were ballads, she cried over *Casablanca* whenever it was on the late show, and her bookcase was full of paperbacks with happy endings. Lovers saying goodbye at the airport made her wistful. Elderly couples who still held hands turned her insides to mush. Weddings brought a lump to her throat. Secretly in the privacy of her home she indulged the sappy side of herself with sachet-scented lingerie drawers, white satin pajamas and bubble baths by candlelight.

Oh, yes, she knew all about romance, knew what it was *supposed* to be, even if she wasn't the kind of woman to inspire it. And Devlin Wingate, with his elegant manners and his easy arrogant charm, was the epitome of romance without even trying to be. She wouldn't stand a chance.

So, no dinner. No matter how much she wanted it.

She stood up, cradling the box of flowers as if it were a baby. "I suppose you have his phone number in that folder of yours?" she said to Vicki.

Silently Vicki scribbled a number on the back of the card that had come with the flowers and handed it to her boss. "You ought to go out with him," she urged, trying one last time. "I bet you'd really enjoy yourself."

"That's what I'm afraid of," Mike said, and disappeared into the privacy of her tiny inner office.

HE ANSWERED THE PHONE on the first ring. "Wingate," he said, his deep voice laced with that thread of an accent that she still couldn't place.

"Mr. Wingate?" Mike began hesitantly, not knowing how to go about thanking a man for the first flowers she had ever received. "This is, uh, Mike Frazer. Your chauffeur?" she added, as if he wouldn't know. "I, uh, I just wanted to thank you for the flowers," she rushed on before he could say anything. "They're beautiful." She glanced over at the open box on her desk, and her voice became more husky than usual. "The most beautiful flowers I've ever seen," she added softly, reaching out to stroke one velvety petal. "I love roses."

There was a slight pause as he digested that bit of information. "I'm glad you like them." Mike heard the clink of ice against glass and wondered what he was drinking. "Does this mean you'll have dinner with me tonight, after all?"

She snapped her attention back to the matter at hand. "Well, actually, no. I, uh, appreciate the invitation but . . . but as I've already told you, Mr. Wingate, it's against company policy for any of the chauffeurs to date customers and—"

"You're the boss. Change the policy."

Mike shook her head. "I can't."

"Sure you can," he said cajolingly. With annoying ease Mike's mind conjured up the teasing smile that accompanied that tone of voice. "Dictate a memo to that secretary of yours. She'll see that everyone gets a copy."

"Mr. Wingate, you don't seem to understand," Mike tried again. "It's not that I *can't*. It's that I don't want to." No, that sounded too harsh. No man liked to be told a woman didn't want to go out with him. Besides, it was a lie. "I mean, well, I'm sorry," she said, trying to soften her refusal, "but dinner is out of the question." Hastily she cast around in her mind for a suitable excuse. "I'm just too busy."

There was a longish pause on the other end of the phone. "I see," Devlin said quietly, a thread of hurt in his voice. "You didn't like the flowers, after all."

"Oh, no, I—" Mike began contritely.

"You probably secretly hate roses and were just trying to let me down easy."

"Oh, no, I love them. Really! They're beautiful. They're the most beautiful roses I've ever seen. They're—"

"Then have dinner with me," he interrupted.

Mike had to laugh, both at herself for taking the bait and at him for dangling it. "Doesn't anybody ever say no to you?" she asked, exasperated.

"No," he said promptly and then laughed with her. The sound poured over her like warm sunlight. "Are you going to be the first?"

"Well, I should," Mike began hesitantly. She wanted to say yes with everything that was in her but was afraid at the same time. A man like Devlin Wingate would be very easy to get used to, very easy to . . . to fall in love with if she let herself. Without even trying, without even knowing it, he was the epitome of every romantic hero she had ever read about, ever dreamed about. It

made her very susceptible and made him very dangerous.

"Have dinner with me," Devlin said, sensing her in-
decision. "I know this great little place on Greenville
called The Grape. Cozy atmosphere. An extensive wine
list. Great cheese board. You'd love it," he coaxed.
"Come with me, Michaelann."

Michaelann. No one ever called her Michaelann.
And he had sent her roses. *Oh, what the hell*, she
thought. *What's one dinner date?* "Yes," she said.

5

"WHAT'S THAT GOOP?" Mike said, eyeing the fluffy mound of white in Vicki's cupped hand with some trepidation.

"Styling mousse. And it won't hurt a bit, so sit still." Vicki rubbed her hands together, then plunged her fingers into Mike's damp hair, ruffling it as she spread the stuff thoroughly. "See? What'd I tell you?" She reached for the blow-dryer that hung beside the bathroom sink, holding Mike where she was by placing one manicured hand on her bare shoulder.

Wordlessly, knowing it was useless to protest and not really wanting to, anyway, Mike tucked the soft green bath towel more firmly around her and watched her short baby-fine hair being shaped into something that actually resembled a hairstyle. Using her fingers as a styling tool, Vicki lifted the sides of Mike's hair up and back, pulling short, random wisps forward to lie in seeming disarray over her forehead. The effect was slightly gamine, slightly sporty, slightly high-fashion punk. It made her wide green eyes, defined with Vicki's charcoal-gray pencil and three layers of carefully applied mascara, look huge.

"Not bad," said Vicki with satisfaction as she surveyed Mike's face in the mirror. "Not bad at all, considering the lack of supplies." She made a face at the small store of cosmetics on Mike's bathroom shelf: mascara, lip gloss, a mostly unused compact of peach-toned blusher and an atomizer of perfume than had been chosen more for its beautiful bottle than its scent. "It's a good thing I always carry my whole arsenal with me." Vicki dropped her bulging makeup case into the open purse on the floor and headed for the closet. "Now for the clothes."

"I thought I'd wear my navy blue suit," Mike ventured, trailing behind Vicki into the bedroom. It was decorated simply in a blend of soft desert hues: silvery sagebrush green mingled with the colors of the sky at sunset. "You know, the one I bought to wear to the bank."

Vicki vetoed that idea with a shake of her head, her pink mouth pursed in disapproval. "I knew I couldn't trust you to do this yourself."

"Why? What's wrong with my blue suit?"

"Nothing, if you're trying to get a loan. But this is a date, remember? Not a business meeting."

"But it's practically brand-new," Mike objected mildly. "I've only worn it three or four times."

"Hmmm, maybe," Vicki agreed absently, her head buried in the depths of Mike's closet as she searched for something she considered appropriate. "But it doesn't have any oomph."

"Oomph?" Mike dropped down on the foot of her bed, a rather dazed look on her face. She had been wearing that expression, on and off, ever since she came out of her office and told Vicki she had a date with

Devlin Wingate. Vicki had taken charge of the situation so fast that Mike almost didn't know what had hit her. She didn't bother to voice a protest; she figured she needed all the help she could get.

"Oomph." Vicki poked her head out of the closet for a moment. "You know, razzle-dazzle. Sex appeal."

"Sex appeal? Me?" A tiny smile turned up the corners of her generous mouth. "In *that* closet?"

"I'll admit, it's tough going," Vicki said, her voice still muffled from inside the closet. "Cotton shirts, jeans, mechanic's coveralls, a couple of suits...no silk blouses, no velvet evening pants, no slinky jersey dresses. Damn! I wish I'd had time to take you shopping before— Hey, wait a minute. Here's something." She emerged with a silky beige shirtdress draped over her arm.

"That?" Mike couldn't believe her secretary was serious. She had worn that dress only once—to her brother Billy Ray's wedding two years ago. The cut was conservative, the color drab and unexciting, but Mike had been in a hurry when she had bought it. Besides, the salesgirl had said it was exactly right for a quiet afternoon wedding.

"Trust me," Vicki said confidently. "You'll look great."

"I don't see how," Mike said mutinously, but she got up from the end of the bed and opened the top drawer of a natural oak chest on the other side of the room. Discarding her towel, she stepped into shimmery yellow panties. Since she rarely wore one, it took her a few seconds to find the matching bra. Vicki's voice stopped her as she started to put it on.

"You don't need that, Mike," she objected mildly. "Your boobs are perfect."

Mike looked at herself in the mirror. From a support standpoint, Vicki was right. Her breasts were small and firm. She didn't really need a bra, and usually she didn't bother to wear one. But usually she was covered up by the heavy material of her mechanic's coveralls or her chauffeur's uniform. Nobody noticed what she was or wasn't wearing under those clothes.

Except Devlin Wingate. He had noticed. His eyes had rested on her unfettered breasts, causing her nipples to tingle and pucker with a sort of nervous excitement. If her body's reaction had been apparent through the material of a denim shirt, it would be doubly apparent beneath the thin silky stuff of her dress.

Mike shook her head at her reflection. "I need it," she said in a voice that brooked no argument. She fastened the front clasp of the bra, tugged a pair of panty hose on and held her hand out for the dress.

It was simple in design, a classic shirtwaist made of a lightweight synthetic that imitated expensive silk. It had wrist-length button-cuff sleeves, a row of tiny buttons up the front and a narrow self-tie belt at the elasticized waist. The dress fit well, skimming over the curve of her breasts, nipping in at the waist, flaring slightly over the gentle swell of her hips. Still, Mike thought the color was unutterably drab, and she wished for the hundredth time that she owned something pink and ruffled and feminine. But she didn't, for the simple reason that pink made her look as though she was suffering from a heat rash, and ruffles made her look like a hayseed dressed in her Sunday best.

"This is sexy?" she said, staring at herself in the long wood-framed cheval mirror that stood next to the oak dresser.

"Hmmm." Vicki walked around her, blue eyes critical as she surveyed the dress. "The color is great on you but—"

"The color?" Mike interrupted. "Are you crazy?" She pinched a fold of the fabric between thumb and forefinger. "There is no color in this dress."

"Oh, there is, too." Vicki brushed Mike's objection aside with the flick of her hand. "It's a lovely light warm beige, and it's perfect on you. It brings out the color of your hair and skin."

"Great!" Mike rolled her eyes. "That's just what I need. Something to bring out my freckles."

"Will you stop?" Vicki chided. "And let me think, please?" She circled Mike again slowly. "It needs something," she said, half to herself. "A scarf or a different belt, maybe." She dove back into the closet again, coming out with a couple of scarves in one hand and a narrow brown snakeskin belt with a small gold buckle in the other. "Let's try these first," she suggested, tossing the belt on the bed as she reached up to loop a green print scarf around Mike's neck. "Don't fidget," she said when Mike began to squirm. "Just stand still."

Silently, her expression communicating exactly what she thought of the whole business, Mike stood still.

Vicki tried one scarf and then the other, tying them this way and that. Neither satisfied her. "You wouldn't happen to have any jewelry, would you? A gold chain or pearls or big hoop earrings or something?" she asked hopefully.

Mike nodded. "I have a gold chain that Harlan gave me for Christmas a couple of years ago." She lifted the lid on a small inlaid box on her dresser. "Would this do?" she asked, holding up a twenty-four inch gold serpentine chain.

"Perfect! Put it on."

Mike complied and then stood still while Vicki went about making the small adjustments necessary to perfecting the outfit. First she flipped up the collar of the dress at the back so that it made a frame for Mike's face and echoed the upswept line of her hair. Then she unbuttoned the cuffs, neatly rolling them halfway up Mike's forearms for a casually elegant look. Next she replaced the self-tie belt with the snakeskin one, defining Mike's narrow waist even more. Lastly she unbuttoned two more buttons on the front of the dress. "There." She stood back to survey her handiwork. "Perfect." She gestured toward the mirror. "Take a look."

Mike looked. And then looked again, entranced by the subtle transformation that had taken place. She wasn't fool enough to believe that she had been turned into a raving beauty by the simple albeit expert application of a few cosmetics and the clever accessorizing of an old dress. She would never be sexy like Vicki, but she did look . . . nice. Yes, that was the word. Nice, and maybe just the tiniest bit elegant in a casual, sporty sort of way.

The hairstyle and makeup made her eyes look bigger and brighter and drew attention to cheekbones that, up until now, she hadn't even known she had. The shirtwaist dress, with its sleeves rolled back and the collar flipped up and the gleaming gold of the necklace lying against the bodice, looked chic and with-it. The narrow snakeskin belt emphasized the slenderness of her waist, subtly drawing attention to the gentle curves above and below it. And Vicki was right: the color *did* do something for her, because even her hated freckles seemed to have faded a bit. She turned from side to side, a pleased little smile turning up the corners of her mouth as she looked at herself in the mirror.

Suddenly a flicker of doubt crossed her face. "You don't think it's too low?" she asked, lifting one hand to cover the hint of freckled cleavage that showed above the buttons that Vicki had undone.

"No way!" Vicki slapped Mike's hand away from the buttons. "You leave it just like that—you hear me?"

Mike still looked uncertain. Exposing her cleavage, slight though it was, seemed somehow brazen, as if she thought it was worth exposing. "But—"

"But nothing," Vicki said, exasperated. "It's perfect. Almost perfect," she corrected herself, disappearing into the bathroom a moment. "Here. Spray a little of this between your boobs and squirt some on the insides of your wrists, too," she ordered, watching to make sure Mike did as she was told. The spicy floral scent of Cinnabar filled the air. "Mmm-mm, nice,"

Vicki commented, taking the bottle from her. She set it on the dresser. "It'll drive him crazy with lust."

"I don't think I want to drive him crazy with lust." She cast Vicki a slightly agonized look. "I wouldn't know what to *do* with him if he were crazy with lust."

"Don't worry about it. I'm sure he knows what to do." Vicki grinned wickedly, her blue eyes twinkling with naughty humor. "In fact, I'd say he's an expert at it."

"Oh, thanks! That makes me feel a whole lot better."

"Well, it should. There's nothing worse than a man who doesn't know what he's doing in bed."

"I'm not going to bed with him!" Mike said, aghast. "This is just a dinner date!"

"Uh-huh."

"Well, it is," Mike insisted. "I only said yes to—"

The doorbell rang, three melodic chimes that echoed through the small town house.

Mike froze, her eyes meeting Vicki's in the mirror. "Ohmigod! He's here!" She glanced around the room as if looking for a way to escape. "What'll I do?"

Vicki grinned. "Put your shoes on," she advised heartlessly. "I'll go let him in."

Mike clutched her arm, stopping her. "No, wait! I'm not ready...I—I've changed my mind. I'm not going out with him." Her fingers pressed into Vicki's arm. "Be a sport, Vicki. Tell him I died."

"No way." Gently Vicki pried her fingers loose and set Mike's hand away from her. "You're going through with this if I have to drag you out there."

"*I can't!*"

"Sure you can," she said cheerfully. "Other women do it all the time."

"But I don't know how."

"Then it's time you learned."

The doorbell rang again.

"Vicki!" Mike pleaded one last time.

"Mike!" Vicki answered in the same tone as she headed for the living room.

Mike stood where she was as if rooted to the spot, listening. She heard the front door open, heard Vicki's voice raised in greeting and Devlin Wingate's lower one answering her. She realized suddenly that her palms were moist.

Ohmigod!

This was worse than the first time she'd had to ask for a loan at the bank, she thought. She had been nervous then, sure: anybody would be nervous in a situation like that. But she'd known exactly what she was going to say and do, known exactly what was expected of her—and what she expected in return.

She didn't have a clue about how to deal with Devlin Wingate, didn't know if she *wanted* to deal with him. She was, at this very minute, sure that she *didn't* want to.

All he wanted—although only God alone knew why!—was her body. Even Vicki said so. "His tongue is hanging out," she'd said, and Vicki knew about those things, so it wasn't just Mike's imagination. Well, that was no problem, she told herself, because he wasn't going to get it. It was obvious that he'd gotten just about everything he'd ever wanted, and she wasn't about to let herself be added to the list.

After all, as she had told Vicki not two minutes ago, this was just a simple dinner date. And she was only going out with him because he'd sent her those beautiful roses, because a date with her seemed to be the only thank-you he would accept. It wasn't as if she really wanted to go.

Mike glanced at herself in the mirror, a guilty flush stealing over her newly discovered cheekbones. It was just a dinner date, and he wasn't going to get . . . she wasn't going to give him . . . anything, she assured herself, looking away.

What on earth had made her say yes to him?

Dinner was bound to last—what? One hour? Two? What would they talk about?

She looked into the mirror again, her eyes accusing as she stared at the slim, chic young woman reflected there. *Impostor,* she thought.

"Mike?" Vicki's voice floated through the bedroom door. "Devlin's here."

It was too late to back out now. "Just a minute," she called, hoping her voice sounded calmer than she felt. *Shoes,* she thought. *I need my shoes. And a purse. Car keys. A comb.* She glanced around a bit wildly, looking for the missing items.

"Mike?"

"Yes . . . yes." She jammed her narrow feet into a pair of shiny low-heeled brown pumps and grabbed a small leather shoulder bag. There was nothing else to do. No good reason to stall any longer. She took one last look in the mirror, her eyes zeroing in uneasily on her exposed cleavage. No sense inviting trouble, she thought, and did up one more button on the front of her dress. Then she gulped once, trying to tamp down the panic in her throat, and took a deep breath. "Yes, I'm coming."

DEVLIN GULPED, TOO, as Mike came out of the hallway into the living room. It was an involuntary reaction, like the sudden flaring of his pupils and the tightening of his stomach muscles. He had told her she was a lovely woman, and he had meant it. But he had been wrong.

She was beautiful.

It wasn't the kind of beauty that shouted to be noticed, like that of her secretary's, nor was it the pampered expensive sleekness achieved by most of the women in his social set. It was something else entirely. Something unstudied and natural and breathtakingly, unconsciously sensual.

The slanting rays of the low-hanging sun spilled through the dining-area window behind her as she hesitated, bathing her in the soft light of early evening. It created a misty red nimbus around her ginger hair and blurred the contours of her dress, making a slim cool taper of her body.

She's like a flame, Devlin thought fancifully, barely able to restrain himself from reaching out to warm his hands, *a living, breathing flame*. And she drew him like a moth, with no rhyme or reason for the intense attraction. The image of her burning beneath him, on fire for him, rose up in his mind again, drawing his stomach muscles even tighter, and he wondered briefly if she'd be hot to his touch. He hoped so. He wanted to be burned by her, with her. He wanted them to go up in flames together.

She moved then, coming forward, and the sunlight streamed through the thin silky stuff of her dress, revealing the rounded contours of her long, firm thighs. The image in his mind became even more precise and graphic. He pictured those long legs wrapped around his hips, pulling him to her in a frenzy of need as strong as his own. Soon, he promised himself.

Mike stopped two feet away from him and held out her right hand. "Mr. Wingate." She greeted him formally, as if he were a business acquaintance, but her welcoming smile was just a bit forced, and there was a tiny flicker of apprehension in her wide green eyes.

The startled doe look, he thought and wondered again what it was about her that made him ache so. It was more than just the red hair. He had dated—and bedded—more than one redhead since Amy Griffen, and not one of them had affected him like this.

He reached out and took Mike's offered hand. "The name is Devlin," he said and raised her hand to his lips as naturally as if he made the gesture every day of his life. "I wish you'd use it."

Standing beside him, watching, Vicki sighed enviously.

Standing in front of him, with his lips touching the back of her hand and his eyes holding hers, Mike melted.

He'd done it again. Without the least shred of self-consciousness or theatrics, he'd fulfilled another of her unspoken romantic fantasies. Nobody kissed a woman's hand anymore, Mike thought dazedly, her eyes gone all soft and dewy. But Devlin Wingate had kissed hers. It turned her bones to jelly and her mind to mush.

"Say 'Devlin'," he ordered softly, his eyes never leaving hers. He was captivated and intrigued by what he saw there. Softness, vulnerability, wonder. She gazed up at him with the eyes of a dreaming child . . . or a love-sated woman who'd been surprised, and pleased, by the ardor of her lover. What was she thinking, he wondered. "Say my name." It was almost a plea.

"Devlin," she murmured obediently. The word was a husky whisper, unconsciously inviting.

Devlin didn't have to be asked twice. He moved forward, his eyes holding hers, his lips seeking. Dreamily Mike lifted her mouth for his kiss.

"Well." Vicki's voice, bright and just a bit too loud, intruded between them. "Well, I guess I'll just get my purse and be on my way."

Mike jumped back as if she had been caught with her hand in the cookie jar. Devlin straightened reluctantly. Vicki hurried in the direction of the bedroom.

Damn, Devlin swore silently. He had almost tasted her lips. Almost. But almost wasn't good enough. Not nearly. "Michaelann," he began, leaning toward her again as soon as Vicki disappeared through the door.

Mike skittered out of his way. "Call me, Mike, please." She flashed him a nervous smile. "Everybody does."

"Mike—"

"Well, here we are." Vicki came sailing out of the bedroom with her purse tucked under her arm. She headed straight for the front door. "I'll just say my goodbyes now."

Mike clutched at her arm as she passed. "Wouldn't you like to stay for a drink?" she asked, sending silent messages with her eyes. *Don't leave me alone with him!* There was no telling what she would do if she was left alone with Devlin Wingate. Throw herself at his feet, probably, and beg him to have his way with her.

"Can't," Vicki said vaguely. "Got things to do."

"Just one?"

"Huh-uh, I—"

"I'm afraid we haven't got time for a drink, either, Mike," Devlin interrupted smoothly, forestalling further excuses. "I made reservations for eight."

"There, you see?" Vicki opened the front door before Devlin could do it for her. "Well, gotta run." She sent Mike a sly little grin. "Don't do anything I wouldn't do," she advised. She hurried down the front steps, her hips swinging under her dress.

The room was very silent. Mike sneaked a quick look at Devlin, eyeing him as though he might jump on her now that they were alone in her living room. She wondered if she would try to stop him if he did. Probably not, she thought.

"Well, shall we?" Devlin tilted his head toward the open door.

"Yes, of course." Mike moved toward the door like a death row inmate who'd been given a reprieve and was heading back to her cell. She halted just inside the threshold, stopping so suddenly that Devlin nearly careered into her from behind. Her new Rolls-Royce Silver Wraith, the pride of her fleet, was sitting at the curb with one of her gray-clad drivers standing beside the open rear door.

"Something wrong?" The words were spoken right next to her ear.

Mike jumped. "Oh, no. It's just . . ." She gestured toward the long silver car, unconsciously sidling away from him at the same time. "You came in my Silver Wraith," she said inanely.

Devlin raised one hand to the doorjamb and leaned forward, making a show of looking around her to the car outside. "So I did." His lips were near her ear again. "What's the matter?" he teased. "Will it violate another regulation if you ride in one of your own limousines?"

"No, of course not. It's just that . . ." Mike drifted off again, not knowing quite what to say. She had never ridden in any of her limousines as a passenger. For evaluation and training purposes, yes: that was part of the whole process of interviewing and hiring a new driver. But never in the back seat as a passenger.

And while she felt that any woman who rode in a limousine was special, the ones who merited the Silver Wraith were even more so. They were brides on their way to the church, high school girls on their way to the Senior Prom, debutantes heading for their coming-out parties at country clubs, wives being treated to a special anniversary present, girlfriends some men were trying hard to impress. Special women, treasured, desired, beautiful.

None of which Mike associated with herself. It came as a shock that Devlin might think of her that way. *Must* think of her that way, since he had gone to the expense of hiring the Silver Wraith for a simple dinner date.

And the flowers, Mike reminded herself. He had sent her those beautiful flowers. He had kissed her hand with all the grace of a true courtier. He had almost kissed her lips. Twice, she reminded herself, thinking of yesterday afternoon at the construction site. He had pursued her relentlessly, until she had agreed to go out with him. And all the while he looked at her as if she were some rare delicacy that he couldn't wait to sink his teeth into. No man had ever looked at her like that before, let alone a man like Devlin Wingate.

She still didn't know why he wanted her, but she believed now that he did. The knowledge heated something deep inside her, something elemental and female, and it welled up, making her feel almost beautiful for the first time in her life. Mike shivered. Such a lovely feeling, feeling beautiful.

"Mike?" Devlin's voice prodded her gently. "Is something wrong? Would you rather I called a taxi?"

Mike turned to look up at him. "No, everything's fine," she said dreamily and smiled into his eyes. The smile lit up her whole face, turning her eyes to gold-flecked emeralds, setting her freckles dancing madly over her cheeks. "Just fine."

She all but floated down the sidewalk to the limousine, leaving Devlin to trail after her with an awed expression on his handsome face.

6

THE RESTAURANT WAS SMALL, the lights were dim, and
the conversation was hushed. They sat in a remote
corner of the room at a tiny table for two with a tray of
cheese and fruit between them and clusters of fat plastic grapes hanging from the latticework overhead.
Music, soft and sentimental, played somewhere in the
background. And Devlin, smiling at Mike over the
sparkle of candlelight and wineglasses, looked more
like a romantic hero than any flesh-and-blood man
should be allowed to.

She hadn't really noticed his attire when he came to
pick her up—not consciously, at least. She'd had too
many other things on her mind. But she noticed it now.
His navy blazer was double-breasted with two rows of
shiny silver buttons and was so dark a blue that it appeared almost black in the dim light. The shirt under it
was a crisp pristine white. His tie was navy with tiny
white pin dots. Mike couldn't see them from where she
sat, but she recalled that his slacks were pale gray, with
razor-creased legs and a fashionably pleated front that
drew attention to the washboard flatness of his stomach.

He looked, Mike thought, as if he belonged on the
deck of a large gleaming yacht, sipping champagne with

a couple of long-legged blondes, but he was sitting right there, less than an arm's length away, smiling at *her*.

Mike sat smiling shyly back at him and feeling as though she had been dropped into the middle of one of her wildest, most romantic dreams.

"Here." Devlin spread some cheese on a thin slice of pear and held it to her lips. "Taste."

Not knowing what else to do, Mike opened her mouth and bit into the succulent slice of fruit. Her eyes downcast, she was careful not to bite too close to the tips of his strong brown fingers. She wondered, though, what they would taste like.

"Like it?"

"Hmmm," she murmured noncommittally, wrinkling up her nose as she swallowed. "What is it?"

Devlin laughed softly at her reaction. "Camembert." He held it under his nose and sniffed deeply. "Aged to perfection."

"It certainly smells, um—" she paused judiciously, searching for a word "—mature."

Devlin laughed again. "I didn't like my first taste of it, either," he said, and popped the remaining half into his own mouth. "But it grows on you if you give it a chance."

"Well, let it grow on *you*, then." She picked up her wine and took a quick swallow, as if to cleanse her mouth of the taste of the cheese. The wine was a new taste to her, too, a young California Beaujolais, Devlin had called it. She wasn't quite sure if she liked it—an ice-cold Lone Star beer or frosty salt-rimmed margarita were more her style—but it was better than the cheese. She took another small sip. Much better, actually.

Devlin grinned at her from across the table and spread some more of the pungent cheese on a small cracker. "Come on," he teased, holding it under her nose. "Where's your sense of adventure?"

Instead of bristling as she had at his earlier teasing, Mike merely smiled and shook her head at him. "I've about used up my sense of adventure for tonight," she said, half to herself. She put her hand on his and pushed his offering back at him. "You eat it."

"Not all of it, I hope," he said and bit into the cracker.

"All of it," Mike admonished playfully. "Didn't your mother teach you to clean your plate?"

"Umm-hmm. I got all the regular lectures. But that's not what I meant." He finished off the cheese-smeared cracker. "I was referring to your sense of adventure."

Mike's brows rose questioningly, her eyes on his over the flicker of the candle flame. Her fingers toyed with the stem of her wineglass.

"You said you'd used up your sense of adventure for tonight," he explained. "I said I hoped you hadn't used up all of it." His lips curved in a sexy, teasing smile. "I have plans for your sense of adventure."

Mike dropped her eyes to the wine in her glass. "Do you?" she asked archly, valiantly trying to play the game.

Devlin gave a low delighted chuckle. "Oh, indeed I do. Definite plans." He put his elbows on the table and leaned across as if he meant to tell her a secret. "Wanna hear 'em?" he whispered.

Mike lifted her shoulders in a tiny shrug, her eyes still downcast as she twisted her wineglass by its narrow stem. How was a woman supposed to answer a question like that? If she said no, she'd be lying. If she said yes, she'd just be asking for trouble. Trouble that she didn't have the least idea of how to handle, even though she wanted to. She kept silent.

"Don't want to answer that, huh?" The laughter was still in his voice. "Okay, answer something else, then."

Mike looked up, still wary but ready to be charmed. "What?"

"What's a nice girl like you doing driving cars for a living?"

"It's a good living," Mike said, instantly indignant at the supposed slur on her profession. "I happen to—"

"I'm sorry—I didn't mean that the way it sounded," Devlin interrupted before she had a chance to get warmed up. "Honest," he added as she continued to scowl at him. "What I really meant to say was 'How did you get started in the limousine business?'" He propped his chin on his hand and smiled at her across the flickering candle flame. It made his gray eyes sparkle like the silver buttons on his blazer. "Tell me the story of your life."

"The story of my life?" Mike repeated. "Why?"

"Because I want to get to know you." He reached out with his free hand and lightly touched her cheek with the tip of one finger. Her skin was warm. Soft. He wondered how it would taste. "Because you fascinate me."

Mike went very, very still. She was used to the gruff affection of her father and brothers: quick embarrassed hugs, teasing pats on the head, a light punch in the arm to express approval. Vicki, the only woman Mike had ever been really close to, expressed her affection with quick little squeezes and pats. And Dan's hands, when he'd touched her in passion, had been selfish and demanding. But no one had ever touched her as Devlin was touching her now; deliberately, as if she were as delicate as one of the roses he had sent her. And no one had *ever* called her fascinating. It made her want to cry or something. Mostly "or something."

"Where were you born?" Devlin asked softly, the backs of his fingers brushing back and forth over her cheek.

"On a farm just outside of Weatherford. That's a—" she faltered as his fingertips drifted down to her jawline "—that's a small town west of Fort Worth."

"And you grew up there?"

"Yes." She felt as if he were hypnotizing her with his touch.

"Brothers? Sisters? Cousins?" he demanded, hungry to know all about her. Where had a woman like this come from? A grown woman, as naturally sensual as any woman he had ever known and who blushed as easily as a young girl being teased by her first boyfriend.

"Just two brothers, both older, and my dad."

"And your mother?"

"She died when I was three."

"I'm sorry." His hand feathered down her shoulder and arm, covering hers where it lay on the snowy tablecloth. "I didn't mean to bring up any unpleasant memories."

"It's all right," Mike reassured him quickly, a little breathlessly, her attention focused on the fingertip that was idly circling the tiny bone on the back of her wrist. "I don't really remember her."

"Still, you must have missed her sometimes."

"Sometimes, I guess," Mike agreed. "But I was basically a happy kid, always busy with one thing or another." She flashed him a quick smile from under her lashes. "There isn't much time to feel sorry for yourself on a farm."

Devlin smiled back and squeezed her hand. "I'll bet you were a cute little tomboy."

"Well," she temporized. "A tomboy, anyway."

"Excuse me, sir. Your mushroom soup." The waitress intruded between them, and Devlin leaned back in his chair, reluctantly moving his hand so that she could put the food down. "And the house salad for the lady."

"You've got to taste this," Devlin said as soon as the waitress had gone. He held a spoonful of mushroom soup to Mike's lips, his other hand cupped underneath to keep it from dripping on the tablecloth. The candle was in the center of the table, between his lifted arms. Its dancing flame flickered over the strong aristocratic features of his face, throwing the sensual contours of his mouth into sharp relief.

Mike wet her own lips, enthralled by the beautiful shape of his.

"Come on," he urged softly when she hesitated. "Open up." He opened his mouth a little, unconsciously imitating the gesture he was coaxing her to make. "It's wonderful stuff."

As she had the last time, Mike opened up. And it was wonderful—both the soup and the fact that Devlin was feeding it to her.

"Isn't that great?" he asked when she had swallowed.

Mike nodded, unable to speak.

"Now," he continued, as if he were totally unaware of the turmoil he had caused in her, "tell me how you went from living on a farm to owning a limousine service."

"Are you sure you want to know? It's not very interesting."

She wasn't being coy, he realized. She really thought he wouldn't find it interesting. What kind of fools had this woman been involved with? "Everything about you is interesting," he assured her. "Tell me."

Maybe he was crazy, she thought, but it was a nice crazy. He seemed as if he really wanted to know. "I've always been interested in anything with an engine," she began. "Ever since I was a little kid. Dad used to let me hang around when he was fixing the tractor or the pickup. Pretty soon I started helping him and—" she shrugged "—by the time I was in junior high I was fixing most of the farm machinery by myself. When I was fifteen, I talked Dad into letting me buy an old '47 MG TC from a neighbor with the money I'd been saving to buy school clothes." A reminiscent grin lit her freckled face. "It only cost me two hundred dollars."

She paused for a second, waiting for a reaction. Most men who had any interest in, or knowledge of, cars at all usually began salivating at the thought of a 1947 MG TC. It was a sports car classic. A perfectly restored one, like her green British racing beauty, was worth many times more than she had paid for it. Devlin merely smiled at her, silently encouraging her to go on with her story.

"It'd been sitting in old man Hotchkin's barn for years," she went on, "all full of hay and nesting chickens. For the next three years that car was my Auto Shop project. I still drive it."

"I didn't know they let girls take Auto Shop."

Mike flashed him a quick little smile. "It was my best subject."

"Hmm." He spooned up the last of his soup. "If I'd known there were girls in Auto Shop, I might've taken the class myself."

"You didn't take Auto Shop? Never?"

"Nope," he said, unrepentant. "I was strictly college prep." He pushed his empty bowl aside. "If my car needs so much as a taillight changed, I take it to a mechanic."

Mike gave a little gurgle of surprised laughter. Most men she knew would never confess to such a thing. It wasn't macho to admit ignorance about something considered as basically "male" as a car. Mike found his unusual attitude refreshing.

"What kind of car do you drive?" she asked curiously. She had a theory that you could tell a lot about a man by the car he drove. Both of her brothers, a farmer and a rodeo cowboy, drove battered pickups. Her banker drove a two-year-old Cadillac. Most of her mechanics drove motorcycles or temperamental souped-up sports cars.

"Depends on where I am." Devlin leaned back again to let the waitress serve his plate of medallions of beef and wild rice. "I keep a Mercedes sedan at the condo here in Dallas. When I'm at the family home in Houston, I drive whatever's gassed up and in the garage. And I have an old army jeep at *mémé*'s summer place on Lake Pontchartrain."

So much for categorizing him by the kind of car he drives, she thought. "*Mémé?*" she prodded, aimlessly pushing her veal in cream sauce around on her plate. "Is she a relative?"

"Lucie Bouvier Wingate, my grandmother." Devlin scooped up a forkful of his wild rice. "Have a taste," he offered, holding it to her lips.

This time Mike didn't even hesitate. Her lips parted, showing the gleam of small white teeth, and then closed delicately over the tines of Devlin's fork. He pulled it away slowly. It was a curiously intimate gesture, one that she couldn't remember ever sharing with anyone else, but it was beginning to feel natural to share it with Devlin.

Everything was beginning to feel natural with Devlin.

"Good?" he questioned. He held her gaze across the candlelight, the fork still poised in the air between them.

She had the strangest feeling that he wasn't talking about the rice.

"Mmm, yes. Delicious," she said, referring not so much to the rice as to the fact that he was feeding it to her. She looked him squarely in the eyes as she said it, but there was a shy uncertain smile on her lips. It was the closest Mike had ever come to flirting with anybody, and she was desperately afraid that it was going to backfire on her. What if he laughed?

Devlin shook his head slowly, disagreeing with her statement. *"You're* delicious," he murmured.

For just a moment, surprise locked her eyes to his, then she blushed with pleasure and ducked her head. No one had ever said anything like that to her before. Never. *He thought she was delicious!* She had no idea how to respond to something like that, and she didn't even try.

Devlin wasn't quite sure how to respond, either. She had reacted to his compliment as though no one had ever given her one before. But that was impossible! She was a beautiful, sexy woman. And it was idiotic to think that she hadn't been told so—repeatedly. And, yet, there was that "startled doe" look of hers, the way her eyes had flared with surprise when he'd told her she was delicious. Her blushes. Her confusion when he'd teased her before. Her nervousness. Was she really as shy as she seemed, he wondered, or was this just some game she was playing to entice him?

He didn't really care either way, he told himself. He wanted her, and if she wanted to play games first, that was fine with him. He liked games. And if she really was as shy as she seemed, well, that was fine, too. Better than fine.

He realized suddenly that he liked a little shyness in a woman; it gave her an appealing touch of vulnerability that attracted the primitive protective male in him. An old-fashioned attitude, maybe, and not one many people would credit him with having, but there it was.

"So," Mike said after a second or two of silence. "Tell me about your grandmother." She pushed her food around on her plate, peeping at him from under her lashes. "Is she French?"

"French Cajun," Devlin corrected with a grin. "And proud of it."

Mike's head came up. "So that's what your accent is!" she crowed triumphantly. "Cajun. I knew you didn't sound entirely Texan."

Devlin paused with his wineglass halfway to his lips. "I don't have an accent."

"Yes, you do. It's very faint and only noticeable on certain words, but it's there."

"Well, I did spend most of my summers with *mémé* and Gramps when I was a kid." He sipped at his wine and then set it down. "And her accent is very pronounced." He grinned again, as if at some private joke. *Mémé's* insistence on flaunting her backwoods Cajun past was a sore spot with Devlin's society-conscious mother and a constant source of amusement to him. His grandmother was a down-to-earth character, his favorite relative, and his mother could be such a snob at times. "In fact, I think she lays it on extra thick sometimes just to drive my mother crazy."

"And you get a kick out of watching her do it." Mike tilted her head consideringly, her lips pursed. "I'll bet you even egg her on sometimes."

"Yeah." His grin widened. "I do. Nobody can ruffle Mother's feathers quite like *mémé*," he said admiringly. "She's a crusty, independent old bird. Always says just what she thinks. About everything. You'd like her." He slanted an assessing look at Mike. "She'd like you, too," he added, realizing as he said it just how true it was. Realizing, too, that it wasn't something he could have said with any degree of honesty to nine-tenths of the women he usually dated. *Mémé* wasn't overly fond of what she called "society hens." "I'll have to arrange a meeting."

Mike made a noncommittal noise that could have been taken for assent. "Is that the extent of your family?" she asked then, remembering Vicki's remark about Devlin being an only son. "Just your grandmother and your parents?"

Devlin shook his head, giving himself time to swallow a bite of marinated beef. "Two sisters. Both younger. You saw one of them the other day."

"I did? Where?"

"When you dropped me off at the condo." He grinned teasingly. "After the flat," he reminded her.

Mike had a sudden vision of the dark-haired young beauty who had hurried out of the high rise that day to greet Devlin. His sister! Of course. She'd had the same glossy black hair, the same golden-olive skin tone, even the same elegant way of holding herself. Something inside Mike lifted, something that she hadn't even known was weighing her down.

"She and Mother were in Dallas for a fitting," Devlin continued, his expression tenderly amused. "Trisha's being decked out as a bridesmaid for the—let's see—for the third time, I think." He speared a piece of beef on his fork. "Another one of her SMU friends," he added as he lifted the fork to Mike's lips. "Would you like a taste of this? The marinade they use here is unique."

Mike cocked her head at him, her green eyes suddenly alight with wry amusement. "Is there some reason you keep trying to feed me?"

"Uh-huh."

Mike waited a second, but he didn't elaborate. "Well?"

"Are you sure you want to know?"

"Of course," Mike said, not sure at all. She was beginning to recognize that teasing light in his gray eyes. And his grin . . . his grin was positively wicked.

"I keep trying to feed you because I like having you eat out of my hand."

She knew she shouldn't have asked. But this time, instead of shyly ducking her head, she met his grin with a teasing little smile of her own. "I think you probably have entirely too many women eating out of your hand already."

Devlin pretended to consider that for a moment. "You're probably right," he said seriously. He held the fork to her lips again. "So . . ." He waggled it back and forth under her nose. "Wanna bite?" he teased.

Her eyes laughing, Mike closed her small white teeth over the cube of meat and tugged it off the fork with a mock-savage jerk of her head.

Devlin's expression turned from teasing to smoldering in an instant. The laughter faded from Mike's eyes. They stared at each other over the candle flame. She swallowed, her slender throat working as the meat went down.

It was suddenly as though, by taking the cube of meat from his fork, she had accepted more than a taste of his dinner. It was as if he had offered more than a forkful of food. It was as if she had just said yes. Yes to anything. Yes, period.

Did she want that? Yes, she realized suddenly, still staring into his eyes. Yes, she wanted it. Wanted him.

Devlin Wingate was the handsomest, most romantic man she had ever met. He conformed to every masculine ideal of romance that she had ever held in the darkest recesses of her secretly, sloppily romantic heart. And somehow, for some reason known only to himself, he wanted her.

He wanted the woman everybody still called "good ol' Mike." Skinny, tomboyish Mike, the one with the red hair and freckles, the girl who hadn't even had a date to the Senior Prom. *And Devlin Wingate wanted her.*

It was utterly amazing, but when Mike looked into his eyes she knew it was true. She could see it smoldering. She could feel it emanating from him in waves of musky male heat. This was the first time anyone had ever wanted her like that, and given her track record, her lack of feminine wiles, it could very well be the last. This might be her only chance to experience all the wonderful things she had only read about.

She'd be a fool to even think of saying no.

"Mike?" Devlin's voice was hesitant, wondering. Her eyes had gone so soft and hot. Almost hungry. He suddenly felt like a lone lamb chop on a plate of parsley. *What in hell was she thinking?*

"Yes?" she said, but it wasn't a question. He knew it and she knew it.

"Are you finished with that?" he asked, nodding toward her plate.

"Yes."

"Would you like anything else? Dessert? Coffee?"

Mike took her courage in two hands, praying that she wasn't making a complete and utter idiot of herself. "Only you," she said softly.

There was total silence for five long seconds as they stared over the flickering candle into each other's eyes. Mike began to think she had made a terrible mistake. Devlin felt like he had been hit in the gut. It took him a moment to recover. Then, without taking his eyes from hers, he signaled for the waitress.

"Check, please," he said, his voice heavy with the sensuality that simmered between them.

Mike let out the breath she hadn't even known she'd been holding. Her instincts had been right; he did want her! She began to tingle all over, trembling like a high-strung Thoroughbred waiting for the starting gate to spring open and set her free.

7

DEVLIN STRUGGLED to hold himself in check during the short ride to his Turtle Creek condominium, intuitively sensing Mike's reluctance to participate in even the mildest form of lovemaking with one of her own drivers in the front seat of the limousine. She might look at him with hot, hungry eyes, she might still be trembling like a leaf in a storm, but she had scooted across the back seat when she got in, leaving a good two feet of plum-colored upholstery between them. Her hands were folded in her lap like a good little girl's at Sunday services. Her face was turned toward the front of the car.

Devlin sighed regretfully. Making love to her in the dimly lit, seductively plush back seat of a moving limousine would have been exciting as hell. Well, he couldn't do that, didn't really want to, if it came right down to it. He wanted more, much more, than a frenzied quickie, no matter how exciting it would be.

But maybe just a kiss or two...or three, he thought. A kiss couldn't hurt. He was dying to taste that luscious mouth of hers. It was full and pink and soft-looking. Just made for kissing.

He moved closer, sliding his arm along the seat behind her head without actually touching her. Mike slanted a flustered look at him out of the corner of her eye and shook her head, glancing nervously toward the chauffeur.

"We could raise the partition," Devlin suggested, his warm breath rustling against her ear. A little privacy could make her feel more relaxed.

"No!" The word was a soft squeak. They could *not* raise the partition. A raised partition meant only one thing when there was a man and a woman in the back seat. Sex. Even if absolutely nothing happened, that was the assumption. She wouldn't be able to look any of her employees in the face tomorrow if she let him raise the partition. *But, oh, how she wanted to let him!*

"You just move right back over there," she whispered, trying to hold on to what last shreds of good sense she had left.

Ignoring her words, he leaned closer; one arm was stretched out behind her head, and his other hand lay flat on the seat between them. Softly he touched her with just his mouth. Just his lips at her ear, plucking delicately at the sensitive lobe as she looked straight ahead, trying to pretend he wasn't doing it. He sighed her name on the soft exhalation of a shaky, heated breath. "Michaelann."

When had anybody ever called her Michaelann in that tone of voice? As if he were dying for want of her?

Her folded hands clenched together in her lap, and she bit her lower lip. What would Doris Day do in a situation like this? Would she tell him to knock it off? What would Vicki do? She choked back a nervous giggle as a picture of her sexy secretary flashed through her mind. No, she couldn't do *that*. Not here in the back seat of her Silver Wraith, with one of her own chauffeurs in the front.

"You move over now," she said weakly, fluttering one hand at him. "Go on."

He pressed his mouth more firmly against her ear and his tongue snaked out to taste the lobe. "I want you, Michaelann." The softly spoken words were a masterpiece of understatement; he had never wanted a woman more.

"Oh." She turned her head sharply, bringing them nose-to-nose. "Oh, I . . ." For the space of a heartbeat they stared at each other, their breaths mingling, lips almost touching. Then she closed her eyes tightly and shook her head. "Not here."

Devlin sighed raggedly. She was right. Not here. Because one kiss or two or even three wouldn't be enough. Because once he got started he wouldn't be able to stop. Not until she was lying naked and sated beneath him.

Willing himself to relax, he leaned back against the seat and reached for her hand. Thankful that he was being reasonable, Mike let him have it without a murmur.

Turning her hand in his, he studied it for a moment, running his fingertip along each slender finger and across her palm as if he were tracing her lifeline. It was a fragile hand, despite the strength he knew it must have, the bones as fine as a bird's. He raised it to his lips and placed a brief hot kiss in her palm.

Mike stiffened as a bolt of pure pleasure shot up her arm.

"No, don't pull away," he said soothingly, misreading her response. "I'll be good now." He placed her hand, palm up, on the seat between them. "Promise," he said, giving it a lingering pat. Then, almost before the last word was out of his mouth, he began softly stroking the center of her palm with his thumb, unconsciously feeding the flames of their growing desire for each other with the slow rhythm of his caress.

Mike gasped softly. Her hand flared open under his, her fingers automatically extending to expose her palm more fully to the stroking of his finger, like a woman's body arching under her lover's touch.

Devlin was instantly aflame again as the desire he had almost succeeded in tamping down burst into brilliant life. He looked up at the small sound she made, his eyes avid and hungry as he sought hers. Mike's glance skittered away, unwilling for him to see how strongly she was affected by such a simple touch. But that didn't keep him from seeing the telltale color that warmed her cheeks.

His eyes raked over her averted face, savoring her betraying blush, and then dropped to the slice of skin revealed by the narrow V of her silky dress. In the dim light afforded by the limousine's courtesy lamps, he could just see the sprinkling of pale reddish freckles that covered her throat and upper chest. The warmth of her blush blended them all together, making her skin look like strawberries whipped into vanilla ice cream. Helplessly drawn, he leaned toward her again, fully intent on taking a bite of her tempting flesh.

The limousine pulled to a stop.

Devlin jerked upright. "Thank God," he mumbled with a heartfelt sigh. Grabbing Mike's hand, he practically dragged her from the back seat. "We won't be needing you any more tonight," he told the driver. He slapped a couple of folded bills into her gloved hand, dismissing her.

And Mike...Mike didn't even care that there would be gossip at the office tomorrow. She was beyond caring or even thinking. Instead, she allowed Devlin to hustle her past the smiling uniformed doorman and into the elevator.

The elevator was brightly lit, and there were two other couples sharing it with them, laughing and chatting about a play they had just seen. The lights and the presence of others effectively put the brakes on Devlin's racing, roiling emotions.

Hold on there a minute, Dev, ol' boy, he said to himself. *Take it easy. She's right here.* He squeezed her waist lightly as if to reassure himself. Mike glanced up at him, smiled shyly and moved a bit closer. *See? She's not going anywhere. So just take it easy.*

By the time they reached his floor, Devlin's little pep talk had had the desired effect. He wouldn't jump on her right away, he promised himself. He'd offer her a drink first.

With that thought firmly in mind, he unlocked the door to the fifteenth floor apartment and ushered her inside. Dropping his keys into a small crystal bowl that sat atop a side table, he turned to offer Mike that drink. But Mike wasn't paying any attention to him just then.

Her eyes had been caught by the extravagant arrangement of tall white flowers in a crystal vase in the center of the narrow side table. The wall behind it was mirrored with beveled panels that reflected back images of the living room at her. She turned to get a better look, her eyes wandering over a long ivory sofa and several plump chairs in shades of taupe and beige arranged around a massive glass coffee table. Silk-shaded brass lamps cast a warm glow over the room, and heavy cream-colored drapes were drawn back over the floor-to-ceiling windows on the far wall, framing the flickering Dallas skyline. There was a wet bar tucked in one corner, gleaming with crystal barware and cut-glass decanters. A muted jewel-toned Oriental carpet graced the floor. Artistically placed bouquets of fresh flowers bloomed everywhere.

Used to it, Devlin didn't give the decor a second glance, but Mike was entranced. Without realizing it, she moved forward to step down two polished marble steps into the huge living room. She felt a little as though she had wandered onto the set of some sophisticated romantic comedy, the sort that Cary Grant always starred in. Everything was elegant and refined, quietly screaming wealth and breeding. Just like the man at her side.

Good Lord, what am I doing here, she thought a bit wildly. She felt way out of her league, like a poor relation who didn't know which fork to use. *I have to be out of my mind to think a man like Devlin Wingate is really interested in me. Totally out of my mind!* Without conscious thought she turned toward the door, intent only on escape.

Devlin was standing right behind her. Chin lifted, he was tugging at the knot of his tie. She halted, mesmerized, as he pulled the knot down enough to flick open the top button on his shirt. That done, he casually shrugged out of his navy blazer and tossed it over the back of the sofa.

"May I take your purse?"

"What?" Mike lifted her head from her contemplation of his bare throat and looked into his eyes. They were still smoldering. Still wanting. She forgot all about leaving between one breath and the next. "Oh, yes, of course."

She dropped her shoulder, intending to slide the long strap of her purse down her arm. The grainy underside of the strap caught at the material of her dress, dragging the fabric away from her neck just as Devlin reached to take the purse from her. His hand grasped her shoulder instead of the purse strap, inadvertently holding her dress askew. His eyes fastened on the exposed curve of her neck and stayed there. His other hand closed over her opposite shoulder, pulling her closer.

"Just one taste," he murmured. "I have to have one taste first." He lowered his head and gently nipped the soft skin of her neck where it started to curve into her shoulder.

Mike gasped. Sharp little fingers of feeling radiated from the place where his mouth touched her skin, sending silent messages of want and need to every part of her body. Her breasts tingled almost painfully. Her thighs trembled and went soft. Her fingers itched to touch him, and she curled them into her palms. Her purse slid unnoticed to the floor.

"Sweet," Devlin murmured. "You're the sweetest..." His lips wandered up the side of her neck, leaving a trail of tiny burning baby kisses in their wake. "The sweetest thing I've ever tasted." He drew back slightly to look into her face. "Do you taste this good all over?" he asked huskily.

Mike's eyes locked with his. Her tongue came out, moistening her suddenly dry lips. "I don't know," she whispered with great daring, "why don't you find out for yourself?"

Devlin tensed for a moment, his stomach tightening, his eyes blazing down into hers. Then he bent, sweeping her into his arms, and went striding down the marble hallway to the bedroom. *The hell with giving her a drink first!*

Mike wrapped her arms around his neck and buried her face against his shirt, praying that she wasn't making the biggest mistake of her life. But it didn't really matter if she was, she told herself. There was nothing she could do about it now. There was nothing she *wanted* to do about it now.

Devlin shouldered open a door, slipped inside a darkened room and came to a halt beside a large satin-covered bed. Mike lifted her head. Slowly, holding her gaze all the while, Devlin let her slide down the length of his body. The only sound was the silky whisper of her dress as it slithered along his clothes and the increased tempo of their breathing. Then her shoes touched the floor, sinking into deep pile carpet, and his arms went all the way around her. She could feel the hardness of his aroused body pressing against the soft flesh of her lower abdomen and instinctively moved closer.

"You are, without a doubt, the most beautiful, the most sensual, the most exciting woman I have ever known," he said, and kissed her.

It was everything Mike had known it would be. His tongue touched the seam of her lips, seeking entry, and then, when she opened to him, delved deeply, searching and hungry, yet taking no more than she was willing to give. And Mike was willing to give it all. It seemed she had been waiting all her life to give everything to this one special man.

Her arms tightened around his neck, pulling him closer. Her lips opened wider under his, offering up the secrets of her mouth to his seeking tongue. They tasted each other thoroughly, yet tentatively, their heads moving and tilting in slow motion as their mouths touched and parted and touched again.

Long, silent minutes passed in mutual exploration, and then Devlin groaned, low in his throat, and pulled back a little. He sighed raggedly and touched his forehead to hers, deliberately slowing their headlong rush into passionate oblivion.

"And to think I was planning to waste time by plying you with liquor," he said teasingly, but his voice was shaky with need.

Mike looked up at him through heavy-lidded half-closed eyes. Her lips were red and shiny from his kiss. "Hmmm?"

"Liquor," he repeated, his eyes raking over her face, taking in each exquisite feature. His hands slid down her back to lock behind her waist. Playfully he rocked her body from side to side. "I was going to ply you with liquor, and then have my wicked way with you."

"You don't need to get me drunk, Devlin." She opened her eyes wider. They were serious and sweet and smoldering, the flecks of gold molten-bright in a surrounding sea of brilliant green. "You can have anything you want without that."

The rocking motion stopped. "Good God, woman, how do you expect me to control myself when you say things like that?"

"But I don't want you to control yourself." Her tone was unconsciously yearning. "I want you to—" Her tongue flicked out nervously, and she floundered, unable to say the words because she didn't know exactly the right words to say.

Devlin placed his finger against her lips. "You don't have to say it," he whispered. "I know what you want. I know." His finger feathered back and forth over her mouth. "I want it, too." His hands moved to frame her face, his palms cupping her cheeks as he gazed down into her eyes. "God, how I want you!" he said fervently and covered her mouth with his.

This kiss was as sweet as the last. No, sweeter, she thought. And hotter. More demanding.

No longer the tentative suitor, Devlin was all aroused male passion. His lips were soft and hot on hers, his tongue ravishing and intimate as he tenderly plundered her mouth. He kissed her thoroughly, expertly, endlessly, his hands still cupping her face, his fingertips gently caressing her earlobes, his body pressing against hers from waist to thigh. Mike sagged against him like a rag doll, helpless to do anything but respond.

As if that were the signal he had been waiting for, Devlin reached between their bodies and found her breast. It was small and delicate in his hand, the soft malleable flesh barely filling the cup of his palm. Her nipple had pebbled against the silky fabric of her bra and dress in unmistakable arousal. Very gently he squeezed it between his fingers. Mike whimpered and pressed into his hand.

He swallowed the sound, overpowering it with his own low growl of desire. "You're so sweet." He sighed against her parted lips. "So responsive." He ran his hand down the curve of her waist to her hip and back up again. "So much passion in such a slender body." He cupped both breasts then, his thumbs stroking lightly over the hardened tips. "And you want me as much as I want you," he said, a note of pleased wonder in his voice, as if he had just been given an unexpected gift.

Mike felt a thrill shiver through her at his words, something distinctly separate from the feeling that his caressing hands induced. Something that warmed her heart as well as her body. Something that freed her passionate, romantic soul. "More," she whispered, greedy as a child who'd just discovered Disneyland.

Devlin chuckled warmly. "Oh, yes. More. Much more," he promised her, dropping a soft kiss on her open mouth. "Just as soon as we get out of these clothes."

Mike gasped at the thought that that conjured up. Devlin, naked. Herself, just as naked. Entwined. For the first time in her life she forgot all about the hated freckles that covered every inch of her body.

But Devlin hadn't.

"I promised myself that I was going to count and kiss every freckle on you," he said, his fingers already busy with the buttons on her dress.

"You want to count my freckles?" Mike struggled to keep her surprise from showing.

"And kiss," he reminded her. "Starting from here—" he pressed a soft kiss against her forehead "—and all the way down to your little pink toes." His white teeth flashed in a wicked smile. "And everything in between. How many do you think there are?"

"I don't know." Mike's voice was a bit dazed. A warm, fuzzy feeling had taken control of her brain. Something hot and tingly was racing along her nerve endings. "Thousands, I guess."

"Good." He slipped the last button free of its buttonhole. "Then it should take me all night." He reached around her to turn on the bedside lamp. Soft amber-tinted light spilled over them. "There. That's better. Now I can see you."

His voice dropped to a husky whisper. "I've been driving myself crazy imagining what you look like under your clothes." He ran one finger up and down between the parted edges of her dress, teasing them both with the feather-light caress. "When you were changing that flat tire, I watched you," he admitted. "There was a little gap in the buttons on your blouse, and every time you moved your arms, I could see the curve of your breast. Right here." His fingertip slipped beneath the fabric of her dress to trace the edge of her bra. "I wanted to touch you then. I wanted to drag you inside that car and tear open your blouse to see if those gorgeous freckles covered all of you."

"F-f-reckles . . ." Mike's voice trembled with emotion. She swallowed and tried again. "Freckles aren't gorgeous."

"Yours are," he said firmly, pushing aside the fabric of her dress. "You have gorgeous freckles. Gorgeous skin." He reached for the front clasp of her bra.

Of their own volition, Mike's hands flew up, stopping him. "No," she said, suddenly shy. "I...that is... You're not getting undressed." She looked up at him through lowered lashes, a delicious blush spreading upward from the exposed tops of her breasts. "Fair's fair."

Devlin dropped his hands to his sides. "Feel free," he invited her.

Mike hesitated for just a second, and then, with fingers that trembled only slightly, she undid his cuffs. She tugged at the knot of his tie and pulled it free. Leaving it to hang around his neck, she reached for the buttons

on his shirt. He wore no undershirt, and his chest was...
Oh, his chest was magnificent!

It was smooth and tanned and hard, with only a
narrow line of silky black hair that started just below
his breastbone and disappeared into the waistband of
his slacks. His ribs were lean, his stomach flat, his male
nipples dark as tarnished copper pennies in the bare
expanse of his tawny chest.

She touched him lightly, experimentally, her fingertips barely skimming over the smooth surface of his
skin. They traveled down his muscled torso, exploring
the shape of him, and feathered across his stomach. His
skin quivered. Mike snatched her hand back.

"Are you stopping there?" His voice was gruff with
the strain of not reaching for her.

Mike shook her head. "No," she whispered. "Oh,
no." The words tumbled out on a tremulous sigh. Taking the edges of his shirt in her hands, she peeled it back
over his shoulders and down the length of his muscled
arms. Impatiently he shook it free of his hands.

"Now it's my turn," he murmured. In seconds she
was standing with the top of her dress hanging around
her waist. Her yellow bra and snakeskin belt lay in a
little heap on the carpeted floor. Her gold serpentine
chain lay gleaming against her heated skin. Slowly
Devlin lifted it off over her head and placed it on the
bedside table. Then he feasted his eyes on her.

"You're beautiful," he breathed, his voice thick with
passion. "Absolutely beautiful."

Her breasts were small and firm with enticing little
tip-tilted nipples that tightened as he looked at them.

He reached out and touched her with his fingers, exploring her as she had explored him. She was freckled all over, every inch of her covered with a lacy veil of color that gave her a warm, inviting glow. And her skin was as hot as he had thought it would be. Hot, and soft as the finest silk. He wanted to touch all of her. See all of her. Taste all of her.

He let his fingers trail around the outer curves of her breasts, down to the bunched material at her waist. Grasping it in his curled fingers, he drew it down over her hips and legs. Mike placed one hand on his bare shoulder for support, kicked off her shoes and stepped out of her clothes. She was naked.

Before she had a chance to think about it, to worry that her small breasts and boyish hips might not be all he could desire, Devlin wrapped his arms around her, pressing her bare breasts to his equally bare chest. The contact electrified them both.

"I knew you'd feel this way against me," he whispered into her ear. "You're so hot. So soft. It's like you're burning me up with the silky touch of your skin." He rubbed his chest against her breasts. "Are you this hot and soft all over?"

"I don't know," Mike said, unconsciously echoing her earlier words. "Why don't you find out for yourself?"

At her words, Devlin leaned down and yanked the blankets back, tossing them off the foot of the bed with careless disregard for the tufted satin spread. A few quick, frantic motions had him as naked as she, and then he lowered them both to the bed, wrapping his arms around her as he nuzzled his face into the curve of her neck.

Mike lay very still, savoring the sensations he evoked. She wanted to lift her hand, to caress his head as he kissed her neck and shoulders, but she couldn't seem to make her body obey her mind's commands. She could only lie there, half covered by his strong lean body, and feel. And what she felt was beautiful.

"Ah, Michaelann." He breathed her name against the soft skin of her neck. "Sweet Michaelann." His mouth wandered lower as he spoke, leaving a damp trail of kisses over her shoulders and chest. "Tell me what you like," he murmured, his lips teasing at the russet crest of her breast. His hand was running up and down the satin length of her thigh. "Tell me what gives you the most pleasure."

Mike made an inarticulate noise in her throat and lifted her hand, pressing his head to her breast. He took the hint and opened his lips, taking her nipple inside the warm wet cavern of his mouth. He worried it gently with his teeth, suckling until she felt the rhythmic tugging pulling at that secret place between her thighs. Her legs shifted restlessly beneath his aimlessly caressing hand. Her fingers tightened in his hair. She whimpered.

"I want to give you more pleasure than you've ever had before, Michaelann," he said, his fingertips dancing over the springy curls at the juncture of her thighs. "Help me. Tell me what you like."

"I . . ." She stiffened, moaning as his hand dipped between her legs. Heat coursed through her at his intimate touch, making her feel as if her blood were on fire. "Oh, that," she panted, breathless. "That."

"Like this?" he whispered. "Is this how you want me to love you?" He stroked her softly, steadily, glorying in her unbridled response.

Mike's head was thrown back against the pillows, her breasts thrust forward, her body arched. "Oh, yes. I . . . like that." She felt as if she were about to explode with the intensity of her feelings. His fingers delved deeper, faster, driving her higher, and she *did* explode. Frantic, she clutched at his shoulders, urging him to cover her, needing the weight of his body to keep her from flying into a million mindless pieces.

Devlin complied eagerly. Balancing himself on his forearms, he settled into the cradle of her thighs. Then, with one smooth controlled thrust, he penetrated the threshold of her femininity. His body stilled in shock.

Michaelann Augusta Frazer was a virgin.

Devlin sucked in his breath, closing his eyes as an intense rush of indescribable pleasure raced through him. *Mine,* he thought triumphantly, vaguely recognizing the pride of conquest, that basic primitive male response to being first, *all mine.* But there was something else there, too. Something deeper and stronger mixed in with the feelings of conquest and soul-searing pleasure. Tenderness flooded him. Tenderness and a ridiculous, inexplicable desire to protect her. But it was too late for that. He had already breached the frail barrier of her virginity.

Carefully he levered himself to his hands without separating himself from the snug warmth of her body.

His expression was anxious and searching as he stared down into her face. Her eyes were closed, her jaw clenched. Was she in pain?

"I'm sorry, Michaelann. I didn't know." He didn't stop to think that there was no way he could have known. "Did I hurt you? Are you all right?" Belatedly he started to draw away from her.

"No!" Mike clutched at his waist, keeping him where he was. "No, don't go. It's all right." There was a breathless little catch in her voice. "I'm all right. It didn't hurt."

"It must have hurt," he insisted, berating himself for his clumsiness. A virgin, no matter how eager, deserved gentler treatment. "I felt something tear when I . . . when I entered you." Gently, almost reverently, he cupped her cheek with his palm. "You flinched."

"That was just surprise." Her hands fluttered up and down his sides, seeking to reassure him, to keep him with her. "That's all. I was just surprised at how it felt."

"I should have been more gentle. Taken it slower."

"No." Mike shook her head against the pillow, denying that there had been any pain. "It was perfect," she whispered. She was smiling as she pulled him back down to her. "Perfect."

And it had been perfect. The pain had been minimal, a slight burning sensation as he had thrust through the barrier, and then his hard warmth had filled her, making her whole. She wouldn't have changed it even if she could have.

She lifted her body invitingly, silently urging him to continue what he had started. Slowly, carefully, Devlin complied. His hips moved against hers, gently at first, mindful of her untried state, and then more strongly as she responded and he became lost in the frenzy of their lovemaking. Mike matched him thrust for thrust, her long legs wrapped tightly around his hips, her body bowed in passionate surrender. Her hands scaled up and down his back, her movements becoming more frantic as he whispered foolish poetic accolades to her beauty and her passion.

"So hot," she heard him gasp between panting breaths. His arms were wrapped tightly around her body, cradling her head and back, holding her as if he couldn't get close enough. "Flame...calling to me. Sweet, sweet Michaelann."

Mike screamed softly as her second climax overtook her.

Devlin reached his own peak a moment later, muffling his groan of pleasure and release in the soft curve of her neck. They both lay unmoving for several long silent minutes, still wrapped in each other's arms, each thinking their own separate thoughts as they waited for the world to right itself around them.

At last, Mike was thinking. *Oh, God, at last!* And it was every bit as wonderful as she had known it would be. All the books were right. The songs. The movies. They hadn't lied about the gloriousness of it. Stars *had* exploded all around her. Bells rang. And the earth was still tilted on its axis. Dan had been wrong. She was capable. All it took was the right man. And she had the right man, right here in her arms. At last.

So that's why I've been acting like such a jackass, Devlin was thinking. The intense immediate attraction he'd felt was no longer a mystery. His almost obsessive desire to be with her, to know her, now had a logical explanation. Even the tender protective feelings that had surfaced when he'd discovered her virginity made perfect sense. Everything made perfect sense.

He was in love. Gloriously, completely, head over heels in love for the first time in his adult life. Just when he had begun to think that it might never happen.

He kissed Mike's neck softly, nuzzling as he breathed in the scent of their spent passion and the lingering whisper of her perfume. And then, never one to waste time once a situation was clear to him, he lifted his head and smiled tenderly into Mike's bemused eyes. "Marry me," he said.

8

"MARRY YOU!" Mike's eyes snapped open, sudden shock replacing the look of bemused contentment. "Did you say *marry you*?"

Devlin nodded lazily and twined a wisp of her hair around his finger. "Yes, marry me."

"Are you *crazy*?"

"I don't think so." He brushed the damp tendril of hair away from her forehead, still smiling that tender fatuous smile as he looked down at her. "Not unless you'd call it crazy for me to be in love with you."

"In love with me? But you can't be in love with me! I— You— We hardly know each other!"

The beginnings of a frown, the merest trace of annoyance, wrinkled his forehead for a moment, then was gone. "I'd say we know each other quite well." He moved his hips against hers lightly, just enough to make his point.

"Well, yes. In the, uh, biblical sense I guess we do but..." Her voice trailed off uncertainly, and she shook her head slightly as if to clear it.

Surely she had heard him wrong. He couldn't possibly have said what she thought he did. She must have misunderstood. But, no, the words had been perfectly clear. *Marry me.* There could be no question about their meaning, could there? Apprehension stiffened her body as a terrible suspicion occurred to her. Surely he wouldn't be so cruel as to tease her about a thing like that?

She looked up into his eyes for a fleeting second, searching for a clue to his true feelings. Devlin smiled lovingly, reassuringly, and brushed at her hair again, smoothing it back from her forehead. Imperceptibly she relaxed.

No, he wasn't teasing her. He was perfectly serious. But why? Why would a man like Devlin Wingate, experienced, worldly, propose marriage after one night with— Her thoughts came to an abrupt halt as sudden comprehension dawned. Ohmigod, of course! Guilt.

It was sweet and chivalrous, and exactly what she should have expected from him, but it wasn't necessary. She staunchly ignored the little voice that urged her to take him up on it—quick—before he changed his mind.

"This isn't Victorian England, you know," she said, her voice a bit prim with the beginnings of embarrassment. "You don't have to atone for...uh, for taking my virginity. And you didn't 'take' it, anyway," she rushed on before he could respond. "I gave it to you."

"And I'm very glad you did. It was a lovely gift." He pressed a soft kiss on her mouth. "A wonderful gift." He kissed her again, making little nibbling motions with his lips. "And I'll be forever grateful that you chose to give it to me. But that's not the reason I asked you to marry me. I asked you because I'm—"

"You didn't ask me," she pointed out quickly, wanting to get this conversation over with. "You told me."

He ignored her interruption. "Because I'm in love with you, not because I feel guilty. Do you think I propose to every virgin I take to bed?"

"Do you take a lot of virgins to bed?" She couldn't help it: the words just slipped out.

"Mike," he said warningly as that slight frown began to wrinkle his forehead again. Dammit, why was she being so contrary? He'd just said he loved her. He'd proposed. And he'd never done *that* before in his life! She was supposed to say she loved him, too. She was supposed to say yes. That's what a woman did when a man asked her to marry him, wasn't it?

Except she was right, he realized: he hadn't asked. He'd told her. And every woman wanted—no, deserved—to be asked. Especially a woman as special as Mike. Besides, *telling* a firebrand like her to do anything would only get her back up. He should have known better.

Devlin's frown cleared, and his expression became one of determinedly loving understanding. "Let's start over, shall we?" He put his hands on either side of her face, gently cupping her cheeks as he looked down at her. "I love you, Michaelann," he said softly, staring into her eyes. "Will you marry me?"

She was almost tempted to take him up on it. He meant it. Any fool could see that. He really did mean it—at the moment, anyway. Just thinking of night after night of the same kind of bliss they'd just shared, of all the little romantic gestures he would treat her to, of all the loving looks and wicked smiles that would be hers, made her start to tremble all over again. He made her tremble. But it wouldn't be fair to take advantage of him this way.

Obviously he was even more of a romantic fool than she was if he could be moved to a proposal of marriage simply because he felt responsible for the fact that she was no longer a virgin. Add to that his obvious state of sexual satisfaction, and it was no wonder that he thought he was in love. But he'd feel differently in the morning. After he'd had time to think about it, he'd probably be shocked that he'd even suggested such a thing, and he'd thank her for turning him down. In the meantime, one of them had to keep things in perspective.

"Devlin." There was a breathy little catch in her voice. "Oh, Devlin." She reached up to touch the backs of his hands where they rested against her cheeks. "I'm flattered. No one's ever proposed to me before. But I can't. I—"

He let go of her face and reared back a little, his arms stiff as he looked down at her. "Are you saying no?"

He sounded so incredulous that she had to smile. "Yes, Devlin, I'm saying no," she said gently.

"Why?" he demanded. Incredulity had rapidly become indignation.

"Because—" Mike floundered for a moment, trying to think of a nice way to put it. But she couldn't think of one. Besides, he was beginning to sound less like a romantic fool and more like a spoiled rich kid who'd been told "no" for the first time in his life. And his frown was back, too, a full-fledged scowl this time. She decided that he didn't deserve a nice answer. "Because the whole idea is ridiculous, that's why."

"Ridiculous!" Devlin rolled off her and sat up. He looked insulted. "I ask you to marry me, tell you I love you, and you say it's ridiculous?"

Mike sat up, too, her ready temper boiling close to the surface at his tone. "That's not love you're feeling. It's lust," she said bluntly, reaching for the pale blue sheet at the foot of the bed. She tucked it over her breasts with quick jerky motions. "You'll forget all about it in the morning."

"You're saying I don't know the difference between love and lust?"

"Obviously!" she snapped, irritated at his tone. "No, no, wait!" She held up her hand, warding him off as he reached for her. One of them had to be reasonable. "Look, I'm sorry. I didn't mean it like that. But, Devlin, think! I'm right, you know. We just made lo—had sex," she corrected herself hastily, "but that's no reason to—"

"You were right the first time," he interrupted. "We made love. At least *I* did." He shot her a huffy, accusing look.

"All right," Mike agreed. "All right. We made love. And it was—" she hesitated over the word for a moment, then plunged recklessly ahead "—wonderful."

"Damn right it was wonderful!"

"And we're both feeling pretty good about it. It's only nat—"

"I *was* feeling pretty good about it. I'm not so sure now."

Mike glared at him but managed to hang on to her temper. "It's only natural that we . . . that you—" She took a deep breath to steady herself and began again. "I mean, I realize that you're feeling responsible or something for my—" She blushed, disconcerted by his unwavering stare. "For the loss of my. . . Oh, dammit, you know what I mean!"

"No." He crossed his arms over his chest and leaned back against the padded headboard, looking down his aristocratic nose at her. "Why don't you tell me what you mean?"

Mike gave him a considering look, half exasperation, half anger. He was reclining against the headboard without a stitch covering him, arms folded, ankles crossed, managing somehow to look as stern and lordly as if he were fully dressed and waiting for an answer from a recalcitrant employee. Mike felt like smacking the expression right off his handsome face. Strangely she also felt like kissing it away. She did neither.

"Look, Devlin, I didn't mean to cast aspersions on your manhood or anything," she said placatingly, belatedly considering the idea that injured pride might be at the core of his bad temper.

She knew enough about men to know that most of them were notoriously touchy about their performance in bed. Her mistake had been in thinking that a man as experienced and skilled as Devlin Wingate would be immune to the malady. Apparently she was wrong. Turning down his proposal of marriage was probably tantamount to saying that she hadn't enjoyed his sexual technique.

"I'm sorry if I hurt your feelings or . . . or made you mad," she continued in the same soothing tone. "But there's absolutely no reason for you to propose marriage. None! We're just two normal healthy adults who were attracted to each other and—"

"Are."

"What?"

"'Are' attracted to each other. You said 'were.'"

"All right. *Are* attracted to each other," she agreed. "And we went to bed together. It was very nice, but—"

"What happened to wonderful?"

Mike's temper snapped. Her green eyes narrowed. Here she was, trying to explain how she felt, and he was making smart remarks. Bruised ego or not, he should at least have the courtesy to listen to her. "All right! It was wonderful! Is that what you want to hear? It was fantastic!" She began to scoot toward the edge of the bed, wrapping the sheet around her as she moved. "Magnificent! The greatest sex I've ever had!"

"It's the *only* sex you've ever had."

Mike didn't hear the sudden thread of humor in his deep voice; she only heard the words. And they made her even angrier. Throw her lack of experience in her face, would he? Her bare feet touched the carpeted floor, and she jumped up, viciously yanking the sheet off the bed as she wrapped it around herself. Her chin thrust outward, hands holding the sheet clutched against her breast, she drew herself up to her full height of five feet eight and a half inches.

"You are the most egotistical, conceited, arrogant man it has ever been my misfortune to meet," she said haughtily, glaring at him. "And I wouldn't marry you if you were the last man on earth!"

"Okay," he agreed instantly, seemingly not at all offended by her dramatic declaration. Laughter hovered around the edges of his mouth. He reached out and grabbed a handful of the sheet that Mike held around her. "How about an affair, then?"

She stood still for just a second, her expression blank as she tried to make sense of his nonsensical words and his sudden change of mood. Then her eyes widened with comprehension, and she pulled back, slapping at his hand in an effort to dislodge it.

"No? You don't want to have an affair, either?" He tightened his grip, winding the pale blue sheet around his wrist as he pulled her closer. Mike was forced to move toward him or lose her covering. "How does a mad weekend fling sound?"

Mike shook her head, refusing to dignify his teasing with an answer. Her arms were pressed tight to her sides, trying to hold the sheet over her breasts. Her hands were engaged in an uneven tug-of-war with his. She might be strong for a woman, but she was no match for even his casual show of strength.

"Don't like that idea either, huh?" He grinned wickedly, his white teeth gleaming in the soft amber light, and yanked hard on the sheet. Mike's knees came against the edge of the bed. "Would you consider a quickie?"

"No! Now let go, dammit!" Mike snapped, valiantly trying to ignore the look in his eyes—and the state of his body. He wasn't mad anymore, or even insulted. He was aroused. Blatantly, fully aroused.

Unwisely Mike released her hold on the sheet to slap at his hand again. The blue material slipped an inch or two lower, exposing one rounded breast. Its tip was puckered tight with quickly burgeoning desire. "Let go, Devlin!" she ordered shakily, struggling as much with the suddenly renewed demands of her own traitorous body as with him.

Devlin shook his head, his eyes riveted on her exposed breast. "Not on your life," he said softly and tugged hard at the slipping sheet, pulling her off balance. His other arm went behind her knees, buckling them.

Mike gave one startled cry and toppled forward, arms outflung to break her fall. She ended up on her back, looking up, with Devlin looming over her like some lecherous god bent on seduction. The sheet lay tangled around her thighs, forgotten.

They stared at each other for a second or two; Devlin's expression was ardent and questioning, Mike's full of wary excitement. Slowly the wariness faded, replaced by a look as warm and knowing as Eve's must have been after the Fall. With a soft breathless sound of surrender, she lifted her arms and looped them around his neck. "Don't you ever take no for an answer?"

"No," he said. And then he kissed her—hard—until they both forgot whatever silly thing it was that they had been arguing about and remembered only that they couldn't seem to get enough of each other.

Love wasn't mentioned again that night. Marriage wasn't even hinted at. And Mike tried to tell herself that she wasn't even a little bit disappointed.

9

"WELL, WELL, WELL. Look what the cat dragged in. Have a good time last night?" Vicki paused, her blond head cocked invitingly, blue eyes speculative as she surveyed her friend and employer.

"Wonderful," Mike answered shortly, determined not to elaborate. She nodded toward the papers spread out on Vicki's desk. "Are those the monthly statements?"

"Almost," Vicki said brightly. "Now quit trying to change the subject. You know I want to hear all about last night," she continued breezily, undeterred by Mike's rudeness. "Was he absolutely wonderful?"

Mike threw herself into a chair in front of her secretary's desk and sank down into her usual sitting position, with one jean-clad leg thrown over the arm. "Got any coffee left in that pot?"

"Of course." With an exaggerated put-upon sigh, Vicki got up to pour Mike a cup. "Hangover?" she asked unsympathetically, handing it over the desk. "Do you need aspirin?"

Mike shook her head, straightening a little as she reached for the fragile china cup. It was translucent white with a narrow silver rim; as classy and elegant as the Silver Wraith. She had chosen the pattern herself to complement the Unicorn Limousine image. "No. I'm fine. No hangover." She smiled, remembering the drink that she *hadn't* had last night. "I'm just a little sleepy."

"Kept you up all night, did he?"

"No, he didn't keep me up all night." Mike took a steadying sip of the fragrant brew. He'd driven her home in his black Mercedes sedan at seven o'clock this morning. She'd had at least four hours sleep before then.

"You kept him up all night?" The waggle of her arched eyebrows left no doubt as to her meaning.

"Vicki!" Both feet hit the floor.

"Well, did you?" she asked, unrepentant.

"No, of course not," Mike said firmly, but the beginnings of a blush gave her away. She buried her face in the coffee cup. It did her no good.

"I knew it!" Vicki crowed, spying the blush. "He took you to his apartment and ravished you, didn't he?"

"He did not *ravish* me." Mike shook her head. "Where in the world do you get words like that?"

"From those books you leave lying all over the place. Well," she prodded when Mike remained silent, "if he didn't ravish you, what did he do?"

A soft secret look lit Mike's eyes, and unknowingly she curved her lips in a satisfied feline smile. For a moment it appeared as if she might say something, but then she shook her head, keeping her thoughts to herself, and took another sip of her coffee.

"That good, huh?" Vicki's voice was just a trifle envious.

"Better." Mike sighed, remembering. "Much better." She looked at Vicki over the rim of her cup, opened her mouth to speak, then closed it again, unable to make up her mind.

"Spit it out," Vicki coaxed. "I know you're just dying to tell me what happened."

Mike hesitated for a second more as her desire to tell someone warred with common sense. It wasn't as if he had meant it; he wouldn't thank her for broadcasting his foolishness. But Vicki was her friend, and she had to tell someone or she'd burst. "He asked me to marry him," she blurted, unable to keep it to herself any longer.

For a moment Vicki didn't say anything. She looked as stunned as Mike had felt when she'd first heard the question. "He asked you to what?"

"Marry him."

"Are you kidding? No, you're not kidding! My God, after one night together? Why?"

"He said he's in love with me."

"After one night?" Vicki repeated, incredulous.

"My sentiments, exactly."

Vicki grinned suddenly, her look of incredulity changing to one of good-natured lasciviousness. "Must have been some night."

Despite herself, Mike grinned back. "It was." She fell silent for a moment, lost in thoughts of just what a night it had been.

"Well, give, girl." Vicki's voice dragged her back to earth. "What did you say when he asked you to marry him?"

"I said no, of course. What else could I say? I told him that we hardly knew each other and that there was absolutely no reason for him to feel responsible for the loss of my virginity. It was my choice, after all, and—"

"Hey, hold on." Vicki held up her hand, palm forward. "Just a minute here. Your *virginity*?"

Mike nodded.

"What about Dan?"

"Oh, Dan." Mike shrugged self-consciously. "I didn't with Dan."

"Obviously," Vicki said dryly. "But why? I mean, I thought Dan was the reason you'd sworn off men. That you were nursing a broken heart, and all. You know, they're all rotten untrustworthy bastards, and you were never going to risk it again."

"Oh, well, I was. But not like that. I mean, Dan did break my heart. Sort of . . ." Her voice trailed off uncertainly. How to explain so that someone like Vicki would understand?

As one of her older brother's rodeo buddies, Dan had been invited to recuperate from a stomping by a Brahma bull at the Frazer farm. Mike, at twenty, had been charmed by his rugged good looks and good ol' boy charm. He'd called her "sweet cakes" and "baby doll" and told her she was "as pretty as a speckled pup." It was pure unadulterated corn, but to a girl who'd never been courted it was heady stuff. She had gladly spent all her limited spare time fetching and carrying for him; plumping pillows, fixing numberless glasses of iced tea, wanting only to be near the first man who had ever paid her the kind of attention that other, prettier, more feminine girls took as their due. It had been only a matter of time before she dropped her guard and let herself fall in love with him. She had thought he was falling in love with her, too, but he wasn't.

When his broken leg mended and his ribs no longer pained him each time he took a deep breath, he changed. He became less charming and more demanding. His kisses were no longer preceded by longing looks and sweet words. His hands were no longer gentle. The courting was over, and he wanted what she had been "promising" him. When Mike balked, he called her a skinny dried-up prude—and worse.

Salvaging his pride by destroying hers, he claimed that he hadn't really wanted her, anyway, that he'd only flirted with her because he felt sorry for her and because there hadn't been anything else to do while he was laid up.

And Mike believed him.

He was, after all, only saying what she already knew herself. And it was time she faced it. She just wasn't the kind of woman who inspired the kind of emotion she wanted to inspire in men. She decided, then and there, that if she couldn't have what she wanted, then she wasn't having any at all.

And that's why she hadn't dated anyone since Dan, and why she had still been a virgin at twenty-four.

"Mike?" Vicki's soft, concerned voice brought her out of her reverie. "Are you all right?"

"What?" Mike shook herself as if coming out of a deep sleep. "Oh, I'm fine. I was just trying to think of a way to tell you about Dan." She paused for a moment, her lips pursed in thought. "Let's just say that I found out what kind of a louse he was after I fell in love with him but before I'd done anything irreversible about it. How's that sound?"

"Fine, I guess. A little surprising in this day and age, but fine."

"Good. I'm glad you approve." Mike reached out and placed her empty cup on the corner of Vicki's desk. "Now, if your prurient interest in my social life has been satisfied, I've got work to do." She stood and stretched her arms above her head for a moment, pulling out the kinks left over from a long night of unaccustomed loving. "I want to have those projections ready for the bank by Monday."

"What for?" Vicki's arched eyebrows rose. "You gave them a pro forma statement when you applied for that loan. What more do they want?"

"Oh, they didn't ask for the projections. But I just thought, what with the new Billings Company account and all, that Arnie might like to see how much faster I'm going to pay the loan off."

"Bankers don't like you to pay off loans early. They lose interest that way."

"Exactly." Mike's husky voice was rich with satisfaction. "And if I can sign even one more corporate account like the Billings Company, they'll lose even more interest." She paused at the door of her office. "In fact, while I'm thinking about it, why don't you get me those files I asked you to put together last week? The ones on prospective clients. It's about time I got off my duff and made some calls."

Vicki brought the files to her less than five minutes later, along with another cup of coffee. Mike murmured her thanks, picked up the coffee and opened the first file, but she didn't read it. She sat there, thinking. About Devlin. About last night.

Marry me, he had said. He might not have really meant it but, oh, it was sweet to hear. She sat at her desk, her hands wrapped around the coffee cup, and allowed herself a brief minute or two of imagining how sweet the reality might be before she reminded herself—again—of all the reasons it was ridiculous.

In the first place, Devlin, as romantic and chivalrous and close to her secret ideal as he was, was still, as Vicki had so aptly put it, the "heir apparent" of a wealthy, socially prominent family. He was practically Texas royalty. And Mike was the tomboy daughter of a small-time country farmer.

Devlin had a condo in the Turtle Creek area of Dallas that looked like something out of *Architectural Digest*, a family home in Houston, a summer place on Lake Pontchartrain in Louisiana, and who knew how many other residences. Mike had a tiny North Dallas town house with a twenty-year mortgage and an open welcome at the whitewashed family farmhouse in Weatherford.

Devlin had a sister who flew to Dallas just to have her bridesmaid dress specially fitted, a mother who "waited lunch" on his arrival and an eccentric French grandmother whom he called *mémé*. Mike had a father and brother who worked dawn to dusk on the farm, a cheerful sister-in-law who bought all her clothes on sale, and a feckless, reckless brother who rode the rodeo circuit.

Devlin wore custom-tailored suits and shirts with French cuffs. Mike's favorite piece of clothing was a worn pair of jeans. Devlin had impeccable manners even when he was being aristocratic and overbearing. Mike's hair-trigger temper was her besetting sin—and she yelled when she got angry. Devlin was far too handsome for his own good and too effortlessly charming for any woman's peace of mind. Mike had red hair and freckles and a figure like an adolescent boy.

And, then, on top of all that, there was his attitude toward business.

Despite his position as president of Wingate Industries, Mike was convinced that Devlin didn't really know the first thing about hard work. How could he, she thought, when the position had undoubtedly been handed to him on a silver platter? Besides, how many real businessmen conducted their day-to-day affairs from the back of a rented limousine—at three times the going rate—just because they were sexually interested in the limousine driver? Not any that she knew of. Not if they wanted to stay businessmen.

She, on the other hand, knew all about hard work and the value of a hard-earned dollar. She'd had to struggle to build her business from scratch: one car at a time; one driver at a time; one client at a time; fighting odds that were stacked against a woman in a predominately male business. But she'd done it. And she loved it.

She loved the smell of grease and the sound of a powerful engine rumbling under a gleaming hood and the last-minute scramble when a driver didn't show up for work or a client called and wanted a car an hour earlier than scheduled. And, nervous as it made her, she loved going into negotiations with her wily old banker and getting what she wanted because she knew what she was doing and she had the facts and figures to back her up.

It was really quite simple. She was a worker. He was a dilettante. They had nothing in common.

Absolutely nothing, she told herself for the umpteenth time, steadfastly ignoring the fierce attraction that had bound them from the minute their eyes had met in the rearview mirror.

But, then, it didn't matter, anyway, because she probably wouldn't even hear from him again now that his desire for her had been slaked. And, even if it hadn't, he'd probably be too embarrassed to contact her after that impulsive proposal he'd made. No, not embarrassed, she corrected herself. She couldn't imagine Devlin Wingate embarrassed about anything. But he might be afraid that she'd change her mind and accept his offer. And then what would he do? Run like a rabbit, probably. And who could blame him? Certainly not her.

She sighed regretfully.

No, she wouldn't hear from him again. The most she could expect would be another dozen roses and a polite note, thanking her for last night, and that would be that.

So stop thinking about him!

She put her coffee cup down with a determined little gesture, clicking it sharply against its saucer, and began to read the neatly typed information in the folder in front of her, willfully blocking out all thoughts of Devlin Wingate.

Vicki had been thorough, as usual, listing every pertinent fact she had come across in her research: company size and age, number of employees, names of key personnel, frequency of out-of-town clients or customers, everything. Mike was soon lost in the facts and figures in front of her, the forgotten coffee cooling at her side. It took a second knock on her office door to drag her attention from the report.

"Mike?" Vicki poked her head around the door. She was grinning like an idiot. "There's someone here to see you."

Carefully Mike marked her place on the page with the tip of her finger. Her heart began to beat a rapid tattoo against the walls of her chest. "Who?"

Vicki shook her head. "Can't tell you. It's a surprise. Do you want to come out here or should he—" Her head disappeared for a moment to check. "Yes, definitely a he—should he come in here?"

"I don't th—" Mike began, but it was too late. Vicki had stepped inside the office, opening the door wide to whoever was outside.

A large valentine-shaped candy box stepped into the room. He had shiny pink arms and legs sticking out of a red lace-trimmed heart body, red satin shoes with curled toes, a red metallic pageboy hairdo and a pink doily hat that looked like the casing from a giant chocolate bonbon. Both hands—in cuffed red gloves—were wrapped around a large crystal vase full of two dozen of the reddest roses Mike had ever seen.

Roses, Mike thought despairingly. Here it comes.

Before she had time to react, the valentine placed the roses on a corner of the desk, executed a courtly little bow and began to dance. The expert soft-shoe routine was accompanied by song. "I've got a message," he sang lustily to the tune of "We're in the Money." He looked ridiculous and whimsical and charming. Mike didn't know whether to laugh or cry.

Vicki was no help. She was leaning against the open office door, giggling. The rest of Mike's employees—all of her mechanics and the few chauffeurs who were on call—were gathered in the outer office, peering in to see what was going on. Mike just sat behind her desk, speechless with surprise and dread and embarrassment, and watched the valentine dance.

He finished with a flourish, bowing grandly from the waist as he held a large heart-sealed envelope toward Mike. She took it, still without speaking, and gave a tiny nod of thanks in return. The valentine bowed again and turned to go. He was met with a burst of spontaneous applause from the group gathered in the outer office.

But Mike just continued to sit at her desk, staring at the envelope as if she could read what was written inside through the thick candy-pink paper. There was nothing on the outside except the shiny red heart-shaped seal and her name, written in red ink.

What was it, she wondered almost fearfully. A thank-you for last night? An invitation? A retraction of his proposal? An excruciatingly polite brush-off?

"Well, don't just sit there like a wart on a frog. Open it."

Mike looked up. The door had closed behind the valentine, leaving only Vicki and herself in the office. Hesitantly Mike slit open the envelope, careful not to damage the red seal. She drew the single square of heavy paper out slowly, convinced that what she was going to read was a polite "thank-you for last night, and I never want to see you again" sort of note. She was wrong.

It's morning and I haven't changed my mind. It wasn't just lust talking. I love you, Michaelann, and I want to marry you. We can discuss the details of the wedding over lunch.

"Oh." One hand fluttered to the region of her thudding heart. "Oh, my," she said breathlessly, staring at what he had written.

"What? What is it?"

"Another proposal." A strangled sound—half delighted laughter, half a snort of disbelief—escaped her. "Or an order. I'm not sure which." She looked up at her secretary, her green eyes brimming with a combination of amazement and amusement and something else that she couldn't quite name. Something dangerously close to joy. "He wants to discuss the wedding details over lunch."

"Wedding details?" Vicki gave her a stern look. "I thought you said you told him no."

"I did but . . ." The joy bubbled up, threatening to overwhelm her. *Devlin Wingate wants to marry me,* she thought gleefully, giving in to it for one heady moment. He wants to marry *me!* She felt like whirling around the room and hugging herself.

"But?" Vicki prodded.

Ruthlessly Mike dragged her soaring spirits back to earth. *We have nothing in common,* she reminded herself. *Nothing.* What she was feeling was just plain foolishness, brought on by the lingering glow of her first sexual experience and the flattering attentions of an attractive man. It meant nothing.

"But Devlin Wingate doesn't seem to understand the word 'no,'" she said as sternly as she could manage. The light of battle brightened her eyes for a moment. She tapped the empty envelope against the palm of her hand. "He's about to learn it, though."

10

"HE JUST PULLED INTO the drive in a big black Mercedes. This year's top of the line," Vicki announced from the outer office. "He's getting out of the car. He's coming this way. No, wait, he's stopped to talk to one of the mechanics. Oh, Lord. Be still, my heart," she said, hurrying over to the open door between the two offices. "He looks like he just walked out of *GQ* Mike. The man is gorgeous. Absolutely gorgeous." She heaved an exaggerated sigh. "And rich. And sexy. And he's crazy about you."

"Crazy, anyway," Mike murmured, her eyes glued to the report she was pretending to read.

"Are you sure you want to do this? Maybe you ought to reconsider."

"I'm sure," Mike said, nervously smoothing her hands over the skirt of her navy suit.

She had rushed home to change after receiving Devlin's message and returned to the office in her going-to-the-bank suit. A tailored white blouse, sensible low-heeled pumps and a soft print scarf knotted into a perky bow tie beneath her chin completed the look of a nononsense executive. The outfit never failed to convince bankers and potential clients of her seriousness;

she counted on its having the same sobering affect on Devlin.

It didn't.

"Hello, sweetheart," he said, breezing into her tiny office without waiting for Vicki to announce him. "Ready for lunch?"

Mike looked up from her desk with what she hoped was an expression of intense preoccupation. "Lunch?" she inquired, as if she had no idea what he was talking about.

Devlin grinned at her, not the least bit abashed. "Yes, lunch." He levered his hip to perch on the corner of her desk, casually hitching up the leg of his gray flannel trousers, and reached for her hand. "You know, that meal that comes between breakfast and dinner. The one that millions of people eat about this time every day." He raised her captured hand to his mouth and gnawed playfully at her knuckles. "Lunch."

Mike's pulse began to race. "About lunch," she began firmly, stubbornly determined to ignore the effect he had on her. It was only physical, anyway, she told herself. It was . . . No, better not to dwell on exactly what it was. She cleared her throat. "About lunch," she said again.

"Yes?" Absently Devlin turned her hand over and kissed the palm, his warm lips moving softly against the sensitive flesh. "You have the sweetest tasting skin," he murmured, as if to himself. "Like sun-warmed strawberries." He looked at her through his black fringe of lashes, head bent as he caressed each slender fingertip with his lips. "Have I told you that?"

"I . . ." Mike's mouth went dry. "Yes, you've told me that," she whispered. Last night, in bed, when his body had been stretched out atop hers and his mouth had been buried between her breasts, he'd told her that.

"Good. I wanted to be sure you knew." He placed one last lingering kiss in her palm. Then, twining her fingers in his, he dropped their clasped hands to his thigh and gave her his full attention. "Now, what did you want to tell me about lunch?"

Mike struggled to remember what it was she had been going to say. Something about not having lunch with him, wasn't it? Something about not marrying him, too. Yes, that was it; she was going to say no.

"I can't have—" she began, and then stopped again, caught by the tender adoring look in his gray eyes and the feel of his hard thigh against the back of her hand.

He had looked at her just like that after they had made love last night. Just exactly like that, as if she were precious and important.

Mike found her resistance wavering under that obviously adoring gaze. What did she want to say no for, anyway? What woman in her right mind would want to say no to Devlin Wingate? *She* certainly didn't want to say no. Not really. What she really wanted was for Devlin to make love to her again. Right now.

Mike stiffened her spine. *You can't have everything you want,* she told herself sternly. Especially when that everything was likely to get you into trouble.

"I'd like to have lunch with you, Devlin," she said then, meaning that part of it with all her heart. "But, as you can see—" she waved her free hand in the direction of the prospective-client files on her desk "—I'm swamped. I haven't got time for lunch today."

"You've got to eat." His voice was soft, persuasive, that sexy Cajun drawl just below the surface, tickling at her nerve endings.

Mike steeled herself against it. "I was planning to have a sandwich at my desk today."

"Fine." He stood up, letting go of her hand as he did so.

Is that it? she wondered, dismayed at his quick capitulation. *Is he giving up that easy?*

"I'll have a sandwich with you."

"You'll what?"

"Have a sandwich with you." He paused halfway across the office, turning to grin at her. "Actually, it's not a sandwich. It's Chicken *en croûte.*"

"Chicken and what?"

"Not 'and'—*en.* Chicken *en croûte.* Boneless breast of chicken smeared with Dijon mustard, wrapped in prosciutto and baked in a puff pastry shell."

Mike just stared at him.

"You'll love it," he assured her. "It's one of my specialties."

"One of your specialties?" It took her a minute to grasp that. "You mean you made it yourself?"

He inclined his head. "With my own two hands."

"Why?"

"Because I thought you might like to drive out into the country and have a picnic. But since you can't—" he turned back toward the door "—I'll just go get the basket, and we can have a picnic in here."

Oh, hell, she thought, feeling her final bit of resistance melting like a snow cone in the Texas sun.

A picnic. He'd brought a picnic for her. And he'd made it himself, actually cooked it himself. With his own two hands. What could be more romantic than a picnic prepared with his own two beautiful well-manicured hands?

Sighing, Mike stood up and reached for her purse. She'd tell him no after lunch. Or during lunch. "Devlin, wait."

Devlin paused in the doorway to look back at her, his expression questioning.

"The paperwork will still be here when I get back," she said, and crossed the room to take the hand he held out to her.

THEY TOOK MIKE'S CAR, the meticulously restored 1947 MG, because Mike preferred to drive herself and Devlin had no macho scruples about being driven by a woman. With the wicker picnic basket and a plaid blanket on the floor between his feet, he directed her to a picnic spot that was several miles out of town. She left the top down, letting the hot summer air whip through the open car as they drove through North Dallas and out beyond the suburbs of Plano and Fairview.

Once they were past the city limits, the land was mostly pasture, broken up here and there by small stands of trees and summer crops of hay and wheat. Fenced-in acreage held cattle or horses. What houses there were, were set far back from the two-lane road. And the road, like most Texas country roads, was straight as an arrow. Gleefully Mike pressed the pedal to the floor, giving in to the ever-present temptation to speed. She loved to drive: the faster, the better.

She glanced over at Devlin to see how he was taking it. He smiled at her, unperturbed. "I think that's our turn coming up," he said, glancing down at the hand-drawn map he had been studying. "Just after the No Trespassing sign."

Mike nodded, downshifting, and slowed the car just a bit. It bumped over the gravel shoulder and onto a narrow dirt road that seemed to go nowhere. Mike braked to a stop. "You sure this is it?"

"Positive," he said. "Past the barn with the blue cow painted on it, turn right at the No Trespassing sign." He motioned her forward. "Drive on, McDuff."

Mike shrugged and put the car in gear. They traveled down the dusty road for another mile or so, open pasture land spreading out on either side of them, until the lane came to an end near a stand of weathered elm trees.

The engine fell silent. The plume of dust plowed up by the car's tires settled behind them. There were no houses in sight, no cattle, no cars. Just silence all around and the fecund smell of the earth under the hot summer sun. The trip from bustling city to peaceful countryside had taken less than forty minutes.

Mike opened her door and got out, waiting by the car while Devlin gathered up the basket and blanket. "Come on. It'll be cooler under the trees," he said, putting a hand under her elbow to lead her to a shady spot beneath the elms.

Mike helped him spread the blanket over the springy cushion of dry buffalo grass and then sank to her knees on it, twisting her body so that she was sitting on her hip, her nylon-clad legs tucked modestly to one side.

It *was* cooler under the trees. Several degrees cooler. Mike had the urge to throw herself backward on the blanket and gaze upward through the leaves at the blue sky beyond, chewing on a stalk of buffalo grass and dreaming of romance as she had done when she was a girl.

Only she didn't have to dream about romance now, she thought, surreptitiously watching Devlin as he laid out the picnic. She was living it right this very minute with a man who embodied every romantic fantasy that she had ever had. He sat just a few feet away, across the width of a blue plaid blanket, pulling crystal wine-glasses and real china plates out of a large wicker basket as if they were in the middle of an English meadow on a cool spring afternoon instead of a North Texas pasture in the dead heat of summer.

Dressed as if he had just walked out of some men's fashion magazine, he wore light gray flannel slacks, a pastel blue-and-white striped shirt left open at the neck and a casually elegant ivory linen jacket with the sleeves pushed up. Fleetingly Mike wished that some benevolent fairy godmother would magically transform her sensible little dress-for-success suit into something more appropriate. A full, gauzy white dress, say, and a big straw hat. One with long trailing ribbons—apple green, she thought whimsically—and white flowers around the crown. And while she was at it, maybe the good fairy could get rid of the freckles, too.

"Here, these are for you," Devlin said, his deep voice calling her from her pleasant fantasy. He held a small bouquet of flowers toward her.

"Oh, Devlin. More flowers." A guilty flush touched her cheeks. "And I haven't even thanked you for the roses you sent this morning. Or the singing valentine, either."

"You can thank me in a minute." A movement of his hand urged her to accept his offering. "Take them."

Mike reached out and plucked the tiny nosegay of violets from his hand. A white paper-lace doily surrounded the deep purple blossoms. Long lavender ribbons trailed from the fragile stems. She lifted the flowers to her face, breathing deeply of their fresh sweet scent. "Oh, Devlin. They're beautiful. Just beautiful."

"They reminded me of you," he said quietly.

Mike's glance caught his over the flowers. "I'm not beau—"

Devlin touched a fingertip to her lips, stopping her words. "Don't argue with me," he ordered softly. A wicked grin etched his face for a moment. "I'm an acknowledged expert on beautiful women. And you're beautiful. Exquisite."

Mike felt her insides melt.

"Now..." His fingers drifted to her chin, tilting it upward. "Where's my thank-you?" He leaned forward.

Mike closed her eyes and met him halfway. Their lips touched softly, parted, touched again, then clung.

Sighing, Devlin curled his hand around her neck and pulled her closer. The kiss deepened: lips parting, tongues seeking. For several long silent minutes more, they kissed, content only to taste each other. Then Devlin's hand wandered to the bow tie at her throat and pulled it loose.

Mike turned her lips from his. "Lunch," she whispered shakily, reminding them both what they had come out here for.

"Umm-hmm. In a minute." He began unfastening the little pearl buttons of her prim white blouse. One button. Two. He ducked his head, touching his lips to the hollow of her throat as his hands slid down to cup her breasts.

Mike sighed, her head falling back, and the hand that held the violets lifted to touch his hair. His lips grazed her collarbone, then drifted lower, nuzzling. The nosegay fell from her fingers, tumbling down his shoulder to the blanket between them. Her hand curled in his thick silky hair. "Devlin." She tugged slightly. "Devlin."

He stilled against her. "Lunch?" he said. She could feel the reluctant laughter rumble in his body.

"Yes." She smoothed his hair, the gesture soothing them both. "Yes, lunch."

"Spoilsport." He sighed heavily and sat up. Plucking the fallen nosegay from the blanket, he tucked it into the open V of her blouse. "To remind me where I left off," he warned her playfully. Then he turned toward the picnic basket and began filling her plate. "I hope you're hungry."

"Starving," she admitted, reaching for the plate he held out to her. "I didn't have time for breakfast this morning."

Devlin looked up from the bottle of champagne he had taken from the basket. "I wonder why?" he said teasingly, that wicked grin of his playing around the corners of his mouth again.

Mike ducked her head at that, pretending a sudden interest in the food on her plate. She could feel the beginnings of a blush heating her cheeks. Resolutely she tried to ignore it, hoping he would, too.

He didn't. "I love it when you blush like that," he said conversationally as he opened the bottle of champagne. "It makes me think of strawberries and vanilla ice cream."

A small pleased smile lit Mike's face for a moment. Then she shook her head at him. "Strawberries again," she commented. "You must be hungry, too." She waved her fork in the direction of his plate. "Eat."

"In a minute." He handed her a champagne flute full of sparkling wine, then poured one for himself. "I want to make a toast first," he said, waiting until she had laid down her plate and lifted her glass to his. "To the future Mrs. Devlin Wingate." He touched his glass to hers and raised it to his lips, watching her over the rim.

Mike was silent for a moment, not sure how to respond. She'd thought that maybe, just maybe, he'd forgotten the whole silly idea, despite the note that came with the roses. Because it *was* a silly idea. It really was. Even if he was in love with her—even if she was in love with him—it wouldn't work. They hardly knew each other. They had nothing in common. They came from two different worlds. They were just two people briefly attracted to each other. Two ships passing in the night. She could see that. Accept it for what it was. Why couldn't he?

"Mike?" Devlin's voice urged her to drink to the toast he had made.

Still she hesitated, frowning slightly, and then sudden inspiration seized her. She raised her glass. "To the future Mrs. Wingate," she said, "whoever she may be." She took a small sip of the champagne, set the glass down on the closed lid of the picnic basket and picked up her plate.

Devlin's expression was wryly amused. "I meant you, you redheaded witch."

"No, you didn't," she said, busily inspecting the food on her plate in order to avoid looking at him.

There was a plump golden pastry, presumably the Chicken *en croûte*, tomato slices in some sort of vinaigrette dressing, and a colorful three-bean salad. Mike liked bean salad. She forked up a bite, found it unexpectedly spicy and reached for her champagne glass. Half the contents disappeared before the fire in her mouth went out.

"What's *in* that?" she gasped when she could talk again. Her eyes were watering.

"A little cayenne pepper and one small green chili. It's three-bean salad, Cajun style." He grinned, unrepentant. "Too hot for you?"

Mike narrowed her eyes at him. "You could have warned me."

"You didn't give me a chance. You were too busy crushing my ego."

"Impossible." She poked at the innocent-looking pastry with the tip of her fork. "Will this take the top of my mouth off, too?"

Devlin shook his head. "It's mostly chicken. Very mild. Just pick it up with your fingers and eat it."

Mike hesitated.

"It isn't going to bite you back, I promise." He took a hearty bite of his own pastry. "See? Harmless."

Still unconvinced, Mike picked hers up in two fingers and nibbled on a corner. It was delicious. They sat munching in companionable silence for a few minutes, and Mike began to hope that he had taken her hint and was going to drop the whole subject of marriage. "Did you really make all this?"

"With my own two hands," Devlin said, refilling their champagne glasses as he spoke. "I can run a vacuum cleaner, too, in a pinch, and I clean up after myself in the bathroom," he added. "I don't leave my dirty socks all over the bedroom floor, either."

"So?" she said, trying to pretend a profound disinterest.

"So, I just thought you should know what kind of husband you're getting."

"I'm not getting any husband at all."

"Oh, yes, you are." He set his empty plate aside, stretched out his legs and leaned back on one elbow. "Me."

"I wish you'd stop saying that."

"Why?"

"Because it isn't true, that's why." She put her plate down and wiped her hands on her napkin. The time had come to tell him no; calmly, coolly, firmly, outright. No. She fixed him with a stern look. "I'm not going to marry you, Devlin. The whole idea is totally ridiculous. And if you'd stop thinking with your . . . your—" her hands fluttered through the air "—glands and start thinking with your head, you'd realize it, too."

"Is it marriage in general you find ridiculous? Or just marriage to me?"

"Marriage to you," she said without thinking. The light in his eyes had her quickly adding, "That is . . . I mean . . . We hardly know each other, Devlin! Four days, that's all. You can't know a person in only four days."

"I know you."

"What?" she challenged. "What do you know about me?"

Devlin finished off the last of his champagne and set the empty glass aside. "I know you're ambitious and independent. I know you work too hard and don't play enough. I know you lost your mother at far too young an age and never had anyone to replace her. No, don't interrupt, there's more," he said, raising his hand to silence her when she would have stopped him. "I know you're stubborn and that you have a temper to match your hair. I know that roses are your favorite flower, that your middle name is Augusta and that you think your freckles are ugly. I also know what nobody else knows—that you're a hopeless romantic and that you like to have the tops of your shoulders kissed there—"

he reached out a long arm and touched her through the fabric of her jacket and blouse "—when I'm making love to you." He cocked an eyebrow at her. "Have I left anything out?"

Mike wet her lips and looked away from his penetrating gaze. "No, but . . ."

"But what?" he coaxed.

She lifted her chin stubbornly, but her eyes were still lowered. "But none of that's important."

He sat up, reaching out to touch her cheek with his fingertips. "There's nothing more important."

Mike shook her head. "Yes, there is. Family. Social position. Attitudes toward business."

"Why, Michaelann Augusta Frazer, you're a snob!"

That brought her eyes to his, gold sparks blazing through the green. "I am not!" she said indignantly.

"You're turning me down because of my family, aren't you? If that's not being a snob, then I don't know what is." There was amusement in his voice—and relief as well. If that was her only real objection, she was as good as his.

"I am not being a snob," she insisted furiously, struggling to get up. The slim skirt and heels made it difficult but she succeeded in pushing herself to her knees.

Devlin grabbed both her hands, sitting her back down with a muted thump. Mike glared at him. "God, you're cute when you're mad," he said cheerfully, infuriating her even further. "All those freckles quivering with indignation and—"

"You leave my freckles out of this!"

"—your eyes shooting sparks hot enough to kill."

Mike shot him a scorching look. "Let go of my hands."

"Not until you promise to sit still and discuss this like a rational human being."

"I have to get back to work."

Devlin shook his head. "Not until we discuss this."

"There's nothing to discuss," Mike said resolutely, tugging to free her hands. "The whole idea is ridiculous."

Devlin shifted his grip, settling her hands more firmly in his. "Just what the hell's so ridiculous about it?" he demanded, starting to get irritated by her continued use of that word. "I'm young and healthy. Reasonably good-looking. I have a solid business reputation. A nice family. No debts to speak of. And—"

"An ego the size of the Grand Canyon."

"—I love you."

Something fluttered in her chest, her heart beating with a tentative joy, but she ignored it. "Right now, you do," she said stubbornly.

"Would you like to tell me what you mean by that?"

"Just what I said. Right now you think you're in love with me. No, that's not right. You've *convinced* yourself you're in love with me because—"

"Mike, I'm thirty-two, not sixteen. That's well past the stage of *thinking* you're in love."

"—because you're too damn stubborn to admit that you made a mistake," she went on, ignoring his interruption.

"Mistake? What mistake?"

"Last night you felt guilty or—" she looked away "—or something about being my first lover and—"

"Dammit, Mike! Don't start that again. I did not feel guilty. Surprised, certainly. And pleased." He let go of one of her hands to turn her face up to his. "Very pleased. But, dammit, not guilty."

"Call it a feeling of responsibility, then." She pulled her chin out of his grasp. "Whatever it was, it made you propose and—"

"I proposed because I love you."

"—when I said no you got stubborn."

"Stubborn? You're calling me stubborn?"

"Yes, stubborn! You're so used to having everybody jump when you tell them to that you just can't believe that anyone would ever say no to you. The word's like a red flag to you. Well, I'm saying no, Devlin. I *have* said no."

"Mike—"

She yanked her hand out of his and struggled to her feet. "Read my lips, Devlin," she said, looking down at him. "No."

There was a long beat of silence. "You're not in love with me," he stated incredulously, as if the thought had never occurred to him before. And it hadn't. Not really. Because how could an emotion that he felt so deeply, right down to the bottom of his soul, not be reciprocated? It was impossible to contemplate. He simply refused to consider the notion.

"I don't know you well enough to be in love with you," Mike said. "And you don't know me well enough to be in love with me, either. Four days isn't—"

"Then what was last night?"

Mike bit her lip. What *was* last night? Honestly? In the cold light of day? "Sex," she answered, reducing what had happened between them down to its most basic form. "Plain old-fashioned biology at work."

That made him mad. "Oh, come on, Mike," he said, jumping to his feet to confront her. "A woman who's guarded her virginity for twenty-four years doesn't suddenly decide to give it up on a first date to a man she hardly knows without a damn good reason."

"I *had* a reason."

"Oh?" His eyebrow lifted imperiously, practically daring her to come up with one.

"Yes! I'd...I'd already decided it was time that I 'gave it up,'" she said, her cheeks pinkening with the lie, "and you just happened to be there."

"Why me?"

"What do you mean, why you?"

"You must know dozens of men; friends, business associates, employees. Why'd you choose me?"

"Because I—" She swallowed. "Because you looked like you'd know what you were doing," she said, remembering a remark that Vicki had made, "and I thought, if I was going to do it anyway, it might as well be with someone who had some experience."

"I see. So you cold-bloodedly decided to go to bed with me."

Her lips pressed together, Mike nodded.

"And when did you make this momentous decision? When you picked me up at the airport? No? Later, then? Perhaps the first time I asked you out to dinner and you said no?" Deliberately casual, he crossed his arms over his chest and leaned back against an elm. "That was a nice touch there, playing hard to get to whet my appetite."

"I was not playing hard to get!"

"Oh? You still hadn't made your decision by then, hmm? Did you make it when you called to thank me for the roses and I had to coax you into saying yes? Or was it when I came to pick you up and you were too scared to come to the door yourself? Or sometime during dinner, maybe, between all those shy glances?"

Furious, Mike could only shake her head.

"No? Not then, either? In the back of the Silver Wraith, when you wouldn't let me kiss you? Wrong again, huh? Well, then, let's see, it must have been later at my apartment." He nodded, as if to himself. "Yes, you must have decided to go to bed with me just after you realized what you'd gotten yourself into and turned around to run."

"I did not run!"

"No, you didn't." He reached out and took hold of her upper arm. "But only because I was between you and the door." His eyes raked over her face. "Only because I kissed you until you couldn't even think of running."

She shook her head again, denying it, and made a halfhearted attempt to twist out of his grasp.

"Admit it, Mike," he said, humor glinting through the passion in his eyes. He got hold of her other arm and pulled her, unresisting, across the little space that separated them. "You made love with me—"

"Had sex," she insisted feebly and laid her hands on his chest. But she didn't push.

"Made love," he corrected firmly. He lowered his head until their lips and their eyes were mere inches apart. "You made love with me because you couldn't help yourself. Because you were on fire. Just like I was," he whispered, his hands caressing her shoulders through the material of her jacket and blouse. "You never made any decision at all, did you? It just happened. Come on, Mike—" his fingers tightened on her shoulders for a moment "—*admit it.*"

"No," she said stubbornly, but her eyes closed and her head tilted back invitingly.

His mouth hovered above hers for a second more, as if he was fighting with himself, and then he was hungrily kissing her. His tongue delved between her parted lips, a marauder, demanding that she give up all her sweetness to his impassioned invasion. His hands tightened on her shoulders, lifting her into him as if he were trying to meld their bodies.

Mike surged upward, her hands curling into the fabric of his linen jacket, and gave herself up to him, unaware of the delicate violets that were being crushed between their straining bodies. The force of his wanting overwhelmed her. Inflamed her. Even last night, when they had been joined in the most intimate way possible, he hadn't kissed her like this. With this degree of want. Of need.

No one had ever wanted her the way Devlin seemed to want her now, and if he had stripped her naked and taken her down to the bare ground, she would have welcomed him. She would have matched his passion with her own.

But his mouth gentled on hers, drawing back to soothe her lips with tiny flicks of his tongue. His hands slid slowly up from her shoulders to her neck and then cradled her head, his thumbs lightly stroking the delicate line of her jaw. She felt him sigh into her mouth, a long shaky sound.

"There's more to this than just sex, Michaelann. For both of us. No, don't deny it." He put a finger to her lips. "Don't say anything."

He kissed her again, softly touching his lips to hers, and then again, more deeply, tilting her head back with his hands in her hair. His tongue took her mouth, slowly, indolently, filling her with the taste and feel of him. She was dazed when he finally lifted his head.

"No woman who stays a virgin until the ripe old age of twenty-four gives herself without feeling something special. Something...important," he said, brushing the feathery curls back from her face as he stared down into her eyes. "It might not be love. Not yet. But it will be."

Gently, almost reverently, he wrapped his arms around her and pressed his lips to her hair. "Just give me a little time, and it *will* be." She felt him breathe deeply, as if he were inhaling her scent, and his arms tightened around her almost painfully. "I'll make you love me."

It sounded like a vow.

11

MIKE HAD BEEN BACK at the office less than an hour when a package arrived for her. Hand delivered, it was wrapped up in deep burgundy paper and pale pink ribbons and bore the scrawling signature of one of Dallas's more exclusive women's boutiques.

Vicki brought it into her office, her blue eyes alive with curiosity as she waited for Mike to open it. "That man has really got it bad," she said, hovering over the desk as Mike untied the ribbon. "And he sure knows how to show it," she added enviously as Mike folded back the cloud of pale pink tissue paper.

Inside lay a soft ivory-colored blouse. Exquisitely and simply tailored with a classic shirt collar, a deep V neck and long button-cuffed sleeves, it was exactly what Mike might have chosen for herself if she had been a more sexually confident woman. It was the right size. It was silk.

The man was . . . amazing, Mike thought, looking down at the faint purple smears on the front of her prim white shirt, left behind by the mangled violets. She had forgotten all about them. Obviously Devlin hadn't.

"I can't accept this," she said, half to herself, as she reached out to touch the mother-of-pearl buttons with the tip of one finger.

"I don't see why not."

Mike looked up at her secretary. "Because it's too personal."

Vicki gave her a disgusted look. "The man is your lover, isn't he?"

Mike shrugged uncomfortably and said nothing.

"Well, isn't he?" Vicki insisted.

Mike nodded, her eyes drawn back to the blouse. She reached out to touch it again.

"Then nothing is 'too personal.'"

"Well, it's too expensive, then," she said stubbornly, her fingers caressing the delicate fabric. "The label says it's pure silk. Silk is expensive, isn't it?"

"Sure, it's expensive. But so what? You wouldn't expect Devlin Wingate to buy some cheap synthetic, would you?"

"No, but—"

"But nothing. Look at it this way. The man's a millionaire. The cost of that blouse—" Vicki waved a hand toward the box "—is no more to him than a . . . a spark plug would be to you."

"That's not the point. I—"

The telephone rang, interrupting whatever she had been going to say. Vicki reached for it automatically.

"Unicorn Limousines," she announced in her best professional secretary's voice. She listened for a second as the caller identified himself. "You have excellent taste, Mr. Wingate," she said, grinning into the receiver. "All right, Devlin, then. Yes, she's right here. Hold on just a minute." She held the phone toward Mike. "It's for you."

"Hello?" Mike said warily.

"Hi, sweetheart." His voice was warm. Caressing. "Miss me yet?"

God, yes, she missed him, but she wasn't about to say so with Vicki hovering over her. She tried to tell herself that she wouldn't have admitted it even if she were alone. "It's been less than two hours, Devlin," she said dryly, more to remind herself of that fact than him.

"Has it? It seems like two days to me."

Mike made a small sound of amused disbelief, trying to think of something to say to that, and her eyes wandered back to the ivory blouse amid its bed of pale pink tissue paper. She really should refuse it. She intended to refuse it. "The blouse is lovely, Devlin," she found herself saying. She caressed the silky fabric with a fingertip. "Really lovely. I don't know how to thank you."

"You could have dinner with me tonight."

"Dinner?"

"Umm-hmm, dinner. You know, the meal that comes after lunch. The one—"

"I know, the one millions of people eat at the same time every day."

"That's it." His low laugh was as intimate as if they were sitting side by side in the back seat of a darkened limousine. "I'll take you out for a steak this time. Someplace casual and country. You can wear your new blouse and those jeans you had on the other day. The ones that look like you were poured into them."

"Devlin! I do not wear—" She paused, catching sight of Vicki's expression of avid interest. "Will you excuse me, please?" she said archly. "No, not you, Devlin. Vicki." She waved her hand. *Go,* she mouthed, motioning the secretary to close the door on her way out. Reluctantly Vicki went.

"And don't wear anything under the blouse," Devlin was saying, his voice low and sexy. "I want to see what you look like with nothing but silk against your skin." His voice got even sexier. "I want to be able to slip my hand inside and touch your bare breast."

Mike swallowed convulsively, blushing as if a hundred other people had heard what he said. This kind of sexy, flirtatious telephone talk was new to her. She was embarrassed and flustered and wildly excited all at the same time.

"Michaelann?"

"Uh-huh." She was clutching the receiver so hard that her hand hurt. "I'm here."

"Are you going to have dinner with me?"

"Yes."

"And wear your jeans?"

"Yes."

"And the blouse?"

"I . . ." She hesitated, wanting to say yes but afraid of what he would think of her if she did.

"Please." The word was as soft and sweet as honeyed butter, and she could almost see the coaxing look that accompanied his tone of voice.

"Yes," she breathed.

"I'll pick you up at your place at eight, okay? We'll go dancing."

"Yes."

"'Bye, sweetheart."

"'Bye," she echoed. Gently, very gently, she laid the receiver back in its cradle. Her heart was beating like a drum, her breathing was shallow and too fast. She felt as if he'd actually put his hand on her.

Ohmigod.

At this rate, she'd never make it through dinner. She'd never make it *until* dinner.

Work. That was it. She had to concentrate on work. Blindly she pulled an open file toward her—one of those she'd left on the desk when she went to lunch with Devlin—and started to read it.

Parker Consulting, she read, forcing herself to concentrate, was an electronics firm that evaluated computer systems and software for other companies. They had lots of out of town clients and did a great deal of entertaining. That made them a perfect prospect for corporate rates and a monthly retainer. She picked up the telephone receiver and dialed.

There, that was done. She had an appointment to speak to the vice president of marketing this coming week. She marked it on her calendar. Now what?

Another file, another phone call, another appointment.

Vicki poked her head in at five o'clock to say that she was leaving for the day. "Hot date," she said, adding that the evening receptionist was already manning the front desk. Mike nodded her goodbye and kept right on talking into the phone. She was on a roll.

By six o'clock she'd made appointments with five different companies. Signing just one would ease her financial headaches considerably. Signing two would give her a nice cushion. Satisfied that she'd done something in the name of business, she locked her desk, tucked the gift-wrapped box under her arm and hurried out to the MG.

Devlin was going to pick her up at eight!

MIKE TOOK A LONG HOT BATH when she got home. She shaved her legs and underarms. She creamed and powdered her body. She washed her hair, blow-drying it into an approximation of the style Vicki had created for her. She made an attempt to duplicate the makeup, too, doing a credible job with the eyeliner and blusher but forgetting to do her mouth.

Giddy as a teenager getting ready for the prom, she even made a small ceremony of getting dressed: stepping into a pair of flowered bikini panties, tugging on pale green knee socks and shimmying into her jeans. Then, feeling somehow wanton and daring in spite of the fact that she habitually went braless, she slipped the blouse on, buttoning it up over nothing except bare skin. It was cool and silky, sliding against her perfumed flesh, and it made her feel very sexy. Very desirable. She tucked the blouse into her jeans, stomped her feet into her fanciest cowboy boots, and was ready.

The doorbell rang. It was eight o'clock on the button.

Mike took a deep breath, grabbed her purse and left the room without even glancing in the mirror. She knew without looking that her nipples were already pushing against the delicate fabric of the silk blouse. The knowledge made her shy as she opened the door.

"Hello, Devlin," she said, not quite daring to look up into his eyes.

"Hello, Mike." She heard him sigh a bit raggedly. "You look lovely. Lovely." He touched her hair lightly, feathering it away from her face at the temple. "But, then, you always do."

That brought her eyes up to his. They were warm with admiration. "Thank you," she said simply, accepting the compliment at face value without looking for any hidden meanings. "So do you. Look nice, I mean." She made a sweeping survey of his elegant frame. "I would never have guessed that you owned such a disreputable thing as a pair of jeans." Her eyes traveled down his long legs to the scuffed boots on his feet. "Or cowboy boots, either."

He raised an eyebrow. "Why not? Every self-respecting Texan owns a pair of jeans and at least one pair of cowboy boots." He took her arm to escort her down the walkway to the car at the curb, shooting her a teasing look out of the corner of his eye. "I think it's a state law."

Maybe, she thought, but not every Texan wore them with a custom-made sport shirt and a raw silk jacket. She opened her mouth to tell him so just as the chauffeur opened the rear door of the car. Chauffeur? Mike blinked, balking as Devlin handed her into the Silver Wraith. He nudged her inside. "Devlin, I don't think..." she began, automatically ducking her head as she slid into the back seat.

He got in beside her. The chauffeur closed the door with a firm click. "Don't think what?" he said, taking hold of her hand as he narrowed the little space between them.

"I—" Mike noticed that the solid partition between the front and back seats was already raised into position. It made the back seat, with its tinted windows and dim lights, a very cozy place. "You shouldn't keep renting this limousine." She scooted over a bit to give him room. "It's expensive."

Casually Devlin closed the gap between them, turning so that he faced her. His arm rested on the seat back behind her head. "I can afford it."

"That's not the point." Unconsciously she edged over a bit more. "No matter how much money you have, you shouldn't go throwing it around. The Mercedes would have been just fine."

"No, it wouldn't." He put his hand on the back of her neck, keeping her from moving any farther.

Mike licked her lips. "Why not?"

"Because I couldn't do this if I were driving the Mercedes." He lowered his head and touched his lips to her cheek. "Or this." He kissed her nose. "Or this." His arms slid around her back, and he sought her mouth with his.

Sighing, Mike put her arms around his neck and kissed him back.

It started out gently, a sweet "hello" sort of kiss. Their lips touched softly, almost tentatively as they explored each other's mouth delicately with the tips of their tongues. It ended with Devlin stretched out atop her, their mouths fused together, his long fingers splayed in her gingery curls, holding her head still for the invasion of his tongue.

Mike's hands were pressed flat against the taut muscles of his back, and her legs had fallen open, cradling his hardened sex against the jean-clad apex of her thighs. Instinctively Devlin pressed forward, moving his hips against hers. Mike whimpered and arched her lower body, her fingers curling around his leather belt to pull him even closer. Her mouth opened wider under his, accepting and encouraging the blatant thrusts of his tongue. Heat swirled around them and between them, building in tempo and intensity, until they had to stop or go all the way.

Devlin groaned and dragged his mouth from hers. "Now tell me you don't love me," he said raggedly. He was breathing as if he had just run a four-minute mile.

Confused, wanting, Mike didn't know what to say. If this feeling was love, if this aching empty need, this terrible want was love, then, yes, she loved him. But was it? Or was it just the repressed desires of a twenty-four-year-old romantic who'd stayed a virgin too long? She didn't know. She had nothing to compare it to.

"No, don't answer that," he whispered before she could gather her thoughts to speak. "Don't answer that. Not yet." His smile in the dim light was rueful and self-deprecating. "I'm sorry. I didn't mean to come at you like that. I didn't mean to push." He brushed back her tousled hair with gentle fingers. "But you go straight to my head, Michaelann. I can't think when I'm kissing you."

When he would have moved off of her, she held him where he was. "I can't think, either," she admitted softly.

He kissed her once more, a quick hard kiss, and levered himself upright. "Thank God for that," he said fervently, pulling her up beside him. "Now." His voice was still a bit shaky. "Let's see what kind of damage I've done." He held her shoulders lightly, peering at her in the dim light. "None," he decided. "You still look lovely." He ran his thumb over her lower lip. "Your lipstick's all gone, though."

Mike's smile was a tiny bit tremulous. "I didn't have any on to begin with."

"Oh. That's all right, then." His hands dropped away from her. "You don't have to do anything before we get there."

Mike nodded, absently smoothing the front of her blouse with her hands. Her heart was still fluttering. "Where's 'there'?" she asked, more for something to say than a real desire to know. She didn't care where they ate dinner, or even if they ate at all.

"The Tumbleweed." He glanced out the tinted window, frowning. "And I think we just passed it. What's the matter with the chauffeur?"

Mike giggled. "As long as the partition's up, she won't stop."

"What?"

"When the solid partition's up—and there's a man and woman in the back seat—it usually means that they're, er, having sex," she explained. She blushed slightly as she said it, but her green eyes were sparkling as they met his. "She'll just keep on driving around the block until it's lowered. It's sort of an unofficial company policy."

"You're kidding!"

"Nope." Mike shook her head. "Next to going through the drive-up window at McDonald's, sex is probably the most popular thing to do in a limousine. Happens all the time." She shot him a flirtatious look without even realizing that she was doing it. "I hope you realize that you've just shot my reputation all to hell. By tomorrow it will be all over the office that I was in the back seat of the Silver Wraith with the partition raised."

Devlin grinned wickedly. "Do you care?"

Mike didn't even think about it. "No," she said, realizing that it was true. She didn't care. "But you'd better lower it, anyway."

He raised an eyebrow at her.

"We're about to pass the restaurant again."

Devlin lowered the partition. The chauffeur glanced in the rearview mirror, confirming that the partition was now down, and turned smoothly into the restaurant parking lot. She opened the rear door, handing them out with absolutely no change of expression.

"She didn't even smirk," Devlin marveled, pushing open the restaurant door so Mike could precede him. The friendly sound of raucous country music and the smell of mesquite broiled steaks drifted out on the night air.

Mike smiled at him over her shoulder. "Of course not. She's from Unicorn Limousines. They're the best in the business."

Devlin chose seats at the back of the large barn of a restaurant, well away from the dance floor and the country-western band. They were good but they were loud, and conversation was easier at a distance. And he wanted to talk to Mike. Just talk to her. It was part of his plan to convince her that they were made for each other.

They both ordered Lone Star beers and T-bone steaks, medium-rare, with an order of sautéed mushrooms on the side.

"I knew we had a lot in common," Devlin remarked when the jean-clad, cowboy-hatted waitress had left.

"What's that?" Mike said absently, tapping her fingers on the checkered tablecloth in time to the music. The tune was upbeat and rowdy, and the Friday night crowd was in full swing on the dance floor.

"Steak, medium-rare. Mushrooms." He indicated her tapping fingers with his beer bottle. "Country music." He grinned at her. "Wanna' dance?"

Mike tilted her head, considering him. "Are you implying that you can do the two-step?" she said skeptically. Cowboy boots or not, he looked like a man who danced to music played by sophisticated combos in classy supper clubs, not rollicking four-piece country bands.

"Are you impugnin' the honor of a Texan, ma'am?" he said with an exaggerated drawl. He laid his hand over his heart. "It's the duty of ever' native Texas male to do the two-step, ma'am. Nay, it is a sacred honor."

Mike pushed her chair back and stood up. "All right, Tex, you're on." She laughed. "But you'd better not step all over my feet."

Devlin grabbed her by the hand, leading her through the packed tables to the equally packed dance floor before she could change her mind. He put one hand on the back of Mike's neck to guide her, took her other hand firmly in his and began to back her around the floor in that gliding, soft-kneed step-step-shuffle-step of the experienced country-western dancer.

"Hey." Mike looked up, impressed. "You really can do the two-step."

"Of course. I can do the Cotton-Eyed Joe, too." He grinned down at her. "I can even waltz if you're not too particular. *Mémé* taught me." He did a tricky little twirl that left her breathless. "Who taught you?"

"My dad, mostly. Sometimes Harlan or Billy Ray would dance with me if there was no one better around."

Devlin smiled down at her. "There *is* no one better," he said.

Mike's eyes were a little misty as she smiled up at him. "You're an awfully nice man, Devlin."

He pulled her closer, slowing their steps to a lazy shuffle. "You're easy to be nice to." He gave her a mock leer. "I'd like to be *very* nice to you."

Giggling, Mike pinched his side. "Be serious."

"I am serious." He pulled her closer still, his hand tightening on the back of her neck until her breasts were touching his chest. He put his lips against her ear. "I would like to be *seriously* nice to you." His tongue snaked out and touched her lobe. "I'd like you to be nice to me, too."

Mike felt her breasts tighten, her nipples pebbling against the friction caused by his shirt rubbing against her blouse. "I'd like to be nice to you, Devlin," she whispered.

"Then what the hell are we doing here?" he growled.

"Having dinner?"

"Right." He let go of her neck and took her by the hand. "Let's go eat before I do something indecent right here on the dance floor."

The waitress slipped their plates onto the table just as they were sitting down. "Another beer, folks?" she asked, picking up the two empty bottles. They both ordered another round.

"So, tell me what you did today," Devlin said, digging into his steak with real gusto.

"You know what I did today. I went on a picnic with you."

Devlin took a sip of his beer. "After that."

"It's not very interesting," Mike said doubtfully, thinking that a man who did as little work as Devlin seemed to do wouldn't find a recital of what she did all day to be very stimulating conversation.

"I told you before, everything about you is interesting."

"Well," she began, warmed and flattered by his attention. "I called up some prospective clients and made appointments for next week. I'm trying to line up a couple of contract customers—you know, on a monthly basis—to clear up a few debts."

"Is Unicorn Limousines in financial trouble?"

"No," Mike said quickly. "It's just that . . . well, I dislike debt of any kind, even when it's necessary. I'm trying to pay off the loan on the Silver Wraith ahead of time."

"Marry me, and I'll pay it off for you." He was only half teasing. He meant it, in one sense. He'd pay off the loan for her, if that's what she wanted, but he didn't seriously expect her to take him up on it.

She didn't. "You don't have to pay for your pleasures," she said tightly, setting her fork down on her plate. "And if that's what you think . . . if that's what you've been trying to do with—" she lowered her eyes to hide the quick hurt "—with your flowers and your presents, then I—"

Instantly contrite, Devlin reached across the table and captured her hand. "That's not what I think, Mike. And you know it. Look at me." He waited until she lifted her eyes to glare at him. God, she was an independent creature. And prickly as hell about it, too. It reminded him of his grandmother. "It was just a joke, sweetheart. Honest."

"A very poor one."

"You're right. And I'm sorry."

She still looked mutinous.

Devlin grinned at her engagingly, rubbing the tip of his finger over the back of her hand. "If it'll make you feel any better, I'll let you buy *my* dinner."

Mike smothered a laugh, charmed in spite of herself. The hurt dissolved as she realized that he hadn't intended to insult her with his thoughtless offer. "Deal," she agreed, smiling at him.

"Good." Relieved to have gotten off the hook so easily, Devlin put his chin in his hand and leaned forward in his chair. "Tell me more about your business," he said. "What kind of clients put you on a monthly contract?"

"Oh, all kinds. For instance, Parker Consulting, one of the businesses I contacted today, is some sort of electronics firm that consults with other businesses about what kind of computer to buy." She was busy cutting the meat on her plate, so she missed the way Devlin suddenly snapped to attention. "Anyway, they have lots of out-of-town clients flying in and out of DFW all the time. Lots of clients they have to wine and dine." She waved her fork in the air. "That sort of thing. Paying us a monthly retainer ends up being cheaper and more convenient *and* much more impressive than rental cars or getting taxis on an as-needed basis. See?" She paused expectantly, waiting for Devlin to comment, and caught him staring at the beer bottle he was twisting against the tablecloth. "Devlin, this really can't be very interesting for you."

Devlin looked up, surprised. "Why not?"

"Well. Because..." She shrugged uncomfortably.

"Come on," he coaxed, intrigued. "Why don't you think I'm interested?"

"Well, you're not even paying attention and..."

"And what?"

"Well, frankly, you just don't strike me as very astute, businesswise."

Devlin burst out laughing. His business astuteness was one of the main reasons the board of directors had named him president of Wingate Industries four years ago. That Mike thought he didn't have any was funny. "Why not?"

Mike pointed her fork at him. "Because, for one thing, you don't seem to actually do any work. I mean," she said, hurrying on, taking his choked expression of mirth for anger, "aside from that first day when I drove you to the construction site, you've done nothing but send me presents and take me out to dinner and on that picnic. I can't see that you've had the time to do any work."

"I was working this afternoon," he said mildly.

"When?"

"On the picnic. What do you think we were doing out in the middle of nowhere?"

"Eating?"

"Yes, but I was also looking over the area."

"What for?" she asked suspiciously.

"A shopping mall."

"A shopping mall?" Her expression was plainly disbelieving. "Out there in the middle of nowhere?"

"It won't be out in the middle of nowhere in ten years. It'll be another bustling suburb of Dallas." He tipped his beer to his lips and looked at her over the bottle. "I gave my lawyers the go-ahead to draw up the initial papers this afternoon. I should be ready to make an offer on the land by Tuesday."

"Oh."

"Now." He set the beer down and leaned across the table. "Don't you feel rotten for having doubted me?"

Mike dropped her chin in mock sorrow and stared down at the checkered tablecloth. "Just terrible," she said, shaking her head with exaggerated remorse.

Devlin leaned closer. "Terrible enough to want to make amends?"

"Such as?" She peered up at him from under her lashes.

He reached out and tilted her chin. "Such as being very, very nice to me for the rest of the evening?"

Mike gave him a slow sweet smile that shook him right down to his boots. Her eyes had a soft sultry look. "I suppose that could be arranged."

12

"CONGRATULATIONS, sweethart." Devlin gave Mike a one-armed bear hug that left her breathless. "I knew you could do it—" He brought his other arm from behind him and wrapped that around her, too. The icy cold of a chilled bottle against the back of her neck sent shivers racing down her spine. "So I brought a little something to celebrate with."

Mike squealed and jumped back, holding out a hand to ward off his smiling advance. "Champagne?" she said, trying to sound disapproving as she retreated behind her desk to avoid the dripping bottle. "Before ten o'clock in the morning?"

"Sure. Champagne's perfect anytime." He put the bottle down on the corner of her desk and began to wrestle with the wire harness on the top. "Especially when you're celebrating a business triumph."

"But how did you know? I got back to the office less than twenty minutes ago." She tilted her head at him. "Do you have spies or something?"

"Or something," he answered, smiling at her as he pushed at the plastic cork with both his thumbs. "I asked Vicki to—" The cork came loose with a surprisingly loud pop, flying halfway across the room as icy bubbles foamed up and over the neck of the bottle.

Quickly Devlin lifted the bottle off the desk to hold it over a wastepaper basket as the foam dripped down his hand instead of all over Mike's papers. "Damn," he said, grinning at her. "I must have jiggled it too much."

Mike grabbed a handful of tissues and mopped at the fizzing liquid before it could stain the starched cuff of his pale blue shirt. "You asked Vicki to what?" she prompted, reminding him of what he had been about to say.

"He asked me to give him a call when you signed Parker Consulting to a monthly retainer," Vicki said, coming into the room with three glasses in one hand and a small plate of petit fours in the other. "So, efficient secretary that I am, I called him as soon as I saw you pull into the driveway."

"And what if I hadn't signed them?" Mike asked, her eyes on Devlin as he handed her a brimming glass. "What then?"

"Then this would have been a consolation prize." Their fingers touched as she took the champagne from him. "But I knew you'd come through with flying colors. If not with Parker, then with some other company. I have complete confidence in you."

He handed the second glass to Vicki and then poured a third for himself. "To success," he said, raising his glass to Mike. She knew from the tone of his voice and the look in his eyes that it wasn't exactly her business success he was toasting. It was success of an entirely different kind he was interested in. His.

"To success," she echoed softly.

The telephone jangled. "Well, back to the salt mines." Vicki sighed regretfully. "I'll just take myself out of here and get that out front." She picked up a decorated petit four in her free hand and headed for the outer office, her hips swaying as she moved. "Have fun, kiddies," she advised, flashing a grin at them over her shoulder. The door closed behind her, and seconds later the phone was silenced in midring.

"Ah, alone at last." Devlin set his champagne glass aside and sank down in the leather armchair behind the desk. With a quick move he reached out and grabbed Mike by the hand. "Come sit on my lap," he said, drawing her onto his knees. He plucked her glass from her hand and set it on the desk behind her as he nuzzled her ear. "We'll play big bad executive takes advantage of the sexy secretary."

"Vicki's the only sexy secretary around here."

He gently bit her ear. "She doesn't hold a candle to you."

Mike giggled and settled into his lap, lifting her arms to wrap them around his neck. The kiss was long and sweet and tasted of champagne. After a moment his hand burrowed under her suit jacket to cup her breast through the material of her blouse.

"Hmmm." Softly, leisurely, Devlin rubbed his lips back and forth over Mike's, leaving them shiny and wet. "I missed you last night," he murmured, moving his head down to nuzzle her throat. Obligingly Mike tilted her head back. "I dreamed that I was making love to you, but when I woke up, you weren't there. It was—" he nipped her collarbone "—frustrating."

"I had to work," she reminded him. "We had that big society wedding booked." Languidly she feathered her fingers through the silky hair at his temples. "Two of my drivers called in sick. I was needed here." She shifted in his embrace, turning slightly to allow him freer access to her body.

"I needed you, too." He slipped open the top button on her blouse, put his hand inside and cupped her breast in his palm. It was bare, small and soft and incredibly sweet. "I need you right now." He pushed her blouse aside with the back of his hand and lifted her breast free. His tongue snaked out, gently touching the puckered tip. "I'll always need you."

Mike sucked in her breath as sensation rushed through her. Unconsciously her fingers curled in his hair. Her breath quickened.

"I swear, Michaelann, you really do taste just like strawberries. Strawberry shortcake." Slowly his tongue stroked her nipple. "Strawberry ice cream." He stroked it again. "Strawberry jam." His lips claimed a nibbling taste of her. "One of these nights I'm going to cover you with whipped cream and gobble you down. Like this." He reached around her body and snagged a pink buttercream rose off one of the petit fours with his fingertip. Carefully he smeared it over her nipple and areola. Then he licked it off.

Mike stiffened as a bolt of pure pleasure knifed through her slender body. Her thighs went slack, moistness gathering in the silky folds between them. Her breasts—the breast he was licking with slow lavish strokes of his tongue—tingled almost painfully.

"Devlin!" Her hands tightened in his hair. "Someone might come in."

"No one would dare," he growled.

"Vicki—" Mike's breath hissed out as his teeth closed gently over her nipple and tugged. "Vicki might need—"

"Vicki least of all." His hand began sliding up under her skirt, seeking the warmth between her thighs. "She knows how I feel about you."

"Devlin." She curled her hands in his hair and pulled his head up from her breast. "Devlin, stop!"

"Why?" The look he turned on her was a bit dazed.

"Because we can't do this here, that's why!"

For a moment she thought he was going to resist, but then he relaxed, his body sagging against hers, his face snuggling into the curve of her shoulder. She could feel the reluctant laughter rumbling in his chest. "No, I guess we can't." His fingertips tiptoed another teasing inch or two up her thigh. "Especially since you're wearing these damn panty hose."

Mike pushed herself upright in his lap. "Panty hose?" she said as she began fumbling around for the buttons on her blouse. "What's the matter with my panty hose?"

Devlin sighed. "I'm going to buy you a garter belt, Mike." He batted her hands away and buttoned up the blouse himself. "A nice little garter belt makes situations like this a whole lot easier."

"What are you talking about?"

"If you'd been wearing a garter belt instead of these panty hose—" he trailed one finger all the way up her leg to the juncture of her thighs and back down to her knee "—the question of 'should we? or shouldn't we?' would be academic by now. We would be." His smile was absolutely decadent. "You'd like making love in a chair."

Mike jumped up off his lap as if she had been stung. "Devlin Wingate, you're depraved."

"And aren't you glad?"

Her smile was slow and sweet and a little surprised. "Yes, I guess I am."

"Yeah?" He patted his lap invitingly. "Then why don't you come back and show me?"

"Oh, no." Mike backed up, putting the width of the desk between them. "I've got lots of work to do today, even if you don't."

Devlin put his hands on the arms of the chair and pushed himself up. "As a matter of fact, I do, too."

"You do?" She made her eyes round with pretended surprise.

Devlin gave her a wry look but otherwise ignored her gibe. "Umm-hmm." Absently he picked up a petit four and popped it into his mouth. "I've got to fly up to Tulsa today to talk to some fool lawyer about an oil lease that he should have been able to handle without my help."

"Then what are you doing here? Why aren't you out at the airport?"

"There's plenty of time." He selected another petit four from the plate. "I wanted to talk to you first."

"Oh, really? Talk?" She slanted him an arch, flirtatious look. "Is *that* what you call it?"

Devlin licked a bit of frosting off his thumb. "Can I help it if I got sidetracked by some wanton hussy who just can't keep her hands off me?"

"Humph." Mike pretended disgust. "You wish."

He grinned at her that arrogant, wicked grin that made him look so appealingly male. "I *know*."

Mike tried hard not to smile back. "Well?" she said, crossing her arms in front of her in an effort to appear stern. "Are you going to tell me what it was you wanted to talk about, or are you just going to keep stuffing your face with those pastries?"

He bit a petit four neatly in half. "I want you to come to Houston with me this weekend. *Mémé* wants to meet you."

Mike went very still. "*Mémé*? You mean your grand—"

Devlin stopped whatever she was going to say by popping the other half of his petit four between her open lips. "She expects us to be there for a little party my mother's giving next Saturday night."

Mike swallowed, lifting her fingers to wipe the sugary crumbs off her mouth. "Saturday night? This coming Saturday night? With your family?" Her skin paled at the thought, making her freckles stand out even more than they usually did. "But, Devlin, won't they think…I mean… Oh, you know what I mean! They'll think that we're, uh, engaged or something, won't they?"

"They'll think you're a beautiful young woman whom I've brought home to meet the family."

"But that usually means . . ." She floundered. "And I haven't agreed to anything. I—"

The buzzer on Mike's desk sounded. "Devlin," Vicki's sweet, sexy voice filled the room. "You asked me to tell you when it was ten-thirty. It's ten-thirty."

Devlin put his hands on Mike's shoulders. "I've got to go, sweetheart, or I'll miss my plane. We'll make our travel plans for Houston when I get back." He pressed a quick hard kiss on her open mouth.

"You planned this." Her green eyes were full of accusation.

"*Mémé* planned it. I told you, she wants to meet you."

"No, I mean you planned to tell me like this, right at the last minute, and then rush off to the airport so I couldn't say no."

"Why should you want to say no?" His expression was innocence personified.

"Because I— Because you— Devlin, there is no reason in the world why I should meet your family." What she really meant was that she was scared to meet them. The Wingates of Houston. It made her shudder to think of it. "Besides, I haven't got anything to wear," she added, as if that settled everything.

Devlin stifled a smile at that. In his experience, when a woman started worrying about what she was going to wear, she was already convinced. He turned toward the door.

"Devlin," Mike said warningly. "I'm not going to Houston."

"I've got a plane to catch, Mike. We'll talk about it when I get back."

"We will not!" she hollered after his departing back.

The sneaky, no-good coward, she fumed to herself.

Thinking he could trick her into going down to Houston to meet his family. She didn't want to meet his family! They would have even less in common than she and Devlin did. She'd tried to tell Devlin before, but he wouldn't listen. What *he* wanted was all that mattered. The selfish swine.

Mike knew exactly what she would find if she went down to Houston with him. A big house with servants, sisters who thought that simply everyone had coming-out parties, a mother who was on every charity fund-raising committee, an aristocratic French grandmother.

She wouldn't fit in.

But would that really be so bad, she wondered. Maybe seeing her with his family, seeing how badly she fit in with them, just might rid him of this crazy idea of marrying her.

And that, after all, was what she wanted . . . wasn't it? Yes, she told herself, of course it was. They were just having an affair. Devlin wasn't in love with her, not really, despite what he said. He was just being stubborn. And chivalrous. The man was a romantic fool, and it would be unfair to take advantage of him.

Besides, she wasn't in love with him. Was she? No, she was . . . infatuated with him. Yes, that was the word. Infatuated. He was her first lover, the first man who had ever sent her flowers and silly singing telegrams, told her she was beautiful, touched her as if she were delicate and precious. He was the first man who had ever desired her—and made her desire him.

And she liked him, too. Most of the time, anyway, she amended, casting a scowling look at the door. He had a whimsical, sometimes bawdy sense of humor that appealed to a side of her she hadn't even known was there. He was polite. Oh, so polite! He was polished. He was elegant and experienced and self-confident. And he made her feel that way, too. He was, in short, everything that a woman's first lover should be. Who wouldn't be infatuated?

But love? No, she didn't think so. Love, real love, was something you *knew*. You either were or you weren't. And she wasn't. Was she? Besides, it would never work.

Sighing, Mike tucked her blouse a little more firmly into the waistband of her skirt and went out into the front office. "Vicki, I need your help."

Vicki looked up expectantly.

"I've been invited to—" How had Devlin put it? "—a 'little' party at Devlin's parents' house. And I don't have anything to wear."

13

THE WHOLE THING was a mistake. Driving down in the MG was a mistake. Meeting Devlin's family was a mistake. The evening dress that she had let Vicki talk her into buying was a mistake. All of it. A mistake. She had known it would be even as she opened her mouth to say she would go to Houston with him.

They had arrived looking windblown and tousled after a four-hour drive in the open car. At least, *she* had been windblown and tousled—and slightly sunburned as well, she thought, touching the tender tip of her nose. Devlin, curse his elegant hide, had looked no more rumpled than if he had been relaxing in the shade all morning, with only a friendly breeze to ruffle his ebony hair.

Thankfully no one rushed out to greet them, giving Mike a chance to surreptitiously pat and tug herself together as she viewed the quietly opulent surroundings and tried to pretend that she wasn't intimidated.

The house was about what she had expected—a white mansion in the classic antebellum style. It had six gleaming columns, three on either side of the massive front door, a wide polished veranda, and a long red brick drive that circled around a two-tiered fountain in front of the house. Except for the well-bred splashing of the fountain behind them as they walked up the steps, it was very quiet, with that insulated hush that seemed to be typical of wealthy neighborhoods. The summer air was heavy and damp, faintly sweet with the fragrance of the flowers in the well-groomed flower beds that flanked the driveway. Somewhere someone was smacking a tennis ball, the muted *thwack* as it hit the strings of the racket punctuating the warm silence.

An elderly white-coated servant opened the front door just as they reached it. "The family is out on the rear veranda, Mr. Devlin," he informed them. "They've been expecting you."

"Thank you, Henry," Devlin murmured politely, giving the man one of his warm charming smiles. "We'll go right out, then." He put his hand on the small of Mike's back, steering her across the wide entry hall, through a sunny room full of flowered sofas and grace-ful cabriole-leg tables, and out through a pair of French doors onto the rear veranda.

It was just like the front veranda, except for the ad-dition of the graceful white wrought-iron furniture with its plump blue cushions, and the two large wooden fans twirling lazily overhead. A manicured lawn ran down from the steps, parted to give way to the tile around a long rectangular pool, and ended at the tennis courts. There was no one playing. The sound of the tennis ball must have come from a neighbor's house, Mike thought as she glanced nervously down the length of the ve-randa.

Devlin's family was gathered at the other end. Like a still life in some glossy magazine, they sat around a glass-topped table set for lunch, blue-flowered place mats and gleaming china at each place. Mrs. Wingate was attired in a soft yellow shirtwaist and pearls, managing somehow to look frosty and elegant in the midst of the humid Houston summer. Two sleek young women, obviously Devlin's sisters, were dressed in tennis togs, their tanned arms and legs gleaming golden against the sparkling white fabric of their clothes. One of them had glossy black hair that tumbled freely to her smooth shoulders; the other, slightly older, confined her ebony mane in a sleek French braid. Mr. Wingate stood at their approach, the newspaper he had been reading held in his left hand. He wore faultlessly creased white slacks and a grass-green polo shirt under a light-weight madras jacket.

Silently Mike cursed her faded jeans and snug-fitting checkered shirt. She had a brand-new pant outfit in her suitcase, one that Vicki had helped her pick out, but she hadn't wanted to wrinkle it with four hours in the car. Now she wished she had. At least then she wouldn't be standing here like Cinderella at the ball, sans the magic of a fairy godmother. She glanced sideways at Devlin, intending to ask him why he hadn't warned her that his family dressed like the people on a resort brochure. But the answer was obvious; it hadn't even crossed his mind. Devlin looked like he belonged on a resort brochure, too.

His mother rose to her feet, both hands extended in greeting as they advanced down the length of the veranda. "We were beginning to wonder where you were." There was a tiny hint of censure in her honey-smooth voice as she offered her cheek to her son. "I've been holding lunch back for the past twenty minutes."

"You should have gone ahead and eaten, Mother," Devlin responded blandly, pushing her chair in for her as she sat down again. "Mike and I would've caught up." He extended his hand across the table to his father. "Dad," he said, nodding at the older man before he turned to introduce Mike to his family. "Mike, I'd like you to meet my father and mother, Robert and Cecilia Wingate."

Mike ducked her head, silently acknowledging the politely murmured hellos.

"This is my sister, Pam."

"Pleased to meet you," Pam drawled softly, her dark eyes skimming consideringly over Mike's slim jean-clad figure, blatantly assessing her. Mike had the distinct impression that the beautiful young woman somehow found her lacking. She lifted her chin a little.

"And my sister, Trisha." Devlin touched the younger woman on the arm, giving her an affectionate squeeze, and she smiled up at her brother before turning curious eyes to Mike.

"Hello," she said politely. Her eyes, too, were assessing, but in a different way.

"Everybody—" Devlin called their attention back to himself, and they all looked up at him expectantly "—this is Michaelann Frazer." He put his arm around her shoulders, hugging her to his side, and grinned happily as he presented her to his family. "The woman I'm going to marry."

Absolute silence greeted his announcement.

Mike didn't know who was more shocked, her or Devlin's family. His family, she decided instantly, taking note of the open-mouthed stares that were being directed at her. At least, she had heard him say it before. They obviously hadn't. *Damn him*. He had all but promised that he wouldn't bring up this silly marriage thing if she would just come and meet his family. And now look what he'd done! She didn't know whether to hit him or crawl into a hole and pull the ground in after her.

"Married?" Cecilia Wingate said faintly. She lifted her hand to her neck as she stared up at her son. "You're getting married, Devlin? To this—" Her disbelieving eyes flickered over to Mike and back "—this . . . young woman?"

"As soon as she sets the date." He squeezed Mike's shoulders again and pressed a quick kiss on her temple.

Mike's body went rigid, but she forced herself to stand still under his arm. *Don't make a scene*, she warned herself. These people would probably hate a scene—and it's just what they would expect of her, too, if the horrified expression in Cecilia Wingate's blue eyes was anything to go by. "He's only kidding, Mrs. Wingate," she said stiffly, glancing up at Devlin through dangerously narrowed eyes. "Aren't you, Devlin?"

"Kidding?" Mrs. Wingate's voice was still faint. "I—" Visibly she struggled to regain her composure. She dropped her hands to her lap and clasped them. "I hardly think marriage is something to kid about, Devlin," she said reprovingly.

"You're right, Mrs. Wingate, it isn't," Mike answered for him. Her cheeks were flushed with anger and embarrassment, her eyes full of gold shards as she glared up at him. "But I'm afraid he's—"

"But I'm not kidding," Devlin interrupted calmly. "I've asked Mike to marry me. Several times."

"And I've said no," Mike snapped. "Several times."

Devlin grinned at his awestruck family. "She's just playing hard to get," he said confidingly.

"I am *not* playing hard to get!" Mike jerked out from under his arm to face him squarely, her chin tilting pugnaciously. "I said no and I meant no. Can't you get that through that thick head of yours? No!" Her voice rose angrily. "I will not marry you. Not now, not—" Mike halted suddenly, her eyes darting sideways. Absolute silence had again fallen over the table. They were all staring at her as if they couldn't believe their eyes. She stood there for a moment more, glaring into Devlin's grinning face, horribly aware that she had been about to make a scene. Just what she'd warned herself not to do. Now what?

Mrs. Wingate stepped smoothly into the breach. "Why don't we all sit down and have lunch?" she suggested, her voice as calm as if nothing had happened. Obviously she had decided to make the best of a bad situation. It was the well-bred thing to do.

Which is fine with me, Mike thought, moving around the table to take the seat that her hostess indicated.

"Michaelann." Cecilia Wingate's tone was questioning. "That's a—" she paused diplomatically, as if searching for just the right word "—an unusual name. I don't think I've ever heard it before."

"It's a combination of my parents' names," Mike offered diffidently, stepping in front of the chair that Devlin pulled out for her. She glared at him over her shoulder as he pushed it in. He answered her with a smirk. Mike decided to ignore him. "Mike and Anna Frazer," she added, speaking to Mrs. Wingate. "But everyone calls me Mi—"

"The name Frazer sounds quite familiar, though," Mrs. Wingate went on smoothly, as if Mike hadn't spoken. "Robert deals with a Frazer in the Midland area. Oil, I think." She glanced at her husband for confirmation. Robert Wingate nodded his head. "Is your family in oil, Miss Frazer?" she inquired, looking at Mike with the eyes of a prosecuting attorney over the centerpiece of full yellow roses.

"No, ma'am. My father's a farmer."

"Wheat?" Mrs. Wingate probed in a further attempt to place Mike in the hierarchy of things. It was apparent from her attitude that she intended to learn all she could about this so-called fiancée of her only son.

"Some wheat," Mike said, uncomfortably aware that Devlin's mother was referring to farming on a much larger scale than her family had anything to do with. "Mostly maize, though. For animal feed."

"Diversification," Devlin's father put in gruffly. "That's the ticket these days."

Cecilia Wingate shot her husband a quelling glance. "Devlin mentioned that you deal in antique cars, Miss

Frazer. That must be fascinating work. You must tell us all about it."

"Well, I—"

"Where's *mémé*?" Devlin interjected, deliberately diverting his mother's attention. Mike would have been grateful if she wasn't so mad at him.

Cecilia Wingate gave an exasperated sigh, momentarily distracted from her cross-examination of Mike. "She called early this morning. Something about one of her dogs going into labor." She grimaced. "She said she was going to stay until the whelping was over."

"Did she say which one? Is it Sadie?" Devlin asked eagerly. Sadie was one of *mémé*'s prize hunting dogs. Lucie Wingate raised some of the best—and most expensive—coonhounds in Louisiana, and Devlin had been promised the pick of Sadie's next litter.

"Really, Devlin, I'm sure I have no idea. You know how your grandmother is." She dismissed the question with a wave of her hand. "Talks like she's got a mouthful of molasses, and she was in a hurry to get back to her dog. I could hardly understand a word she said."

She glanced up at the man who had just come out onto the veranda. "Thank you, Henry," she said to the silent servant as he placed a large silver tray of crustless sandwiches on the table. "You can put that right there—" she directed his placement of a lavish relish tray "—and then bring out the fruit compote. And we'll need more iced tea, too, please." She glanced over at Mike. "Unless you'd like something else, Miss Frazer?" There was the tiniest bit of challenge in her eyes, Mike thought, as if she were expecting Mike to be ill-bred enough to ask for something that wasn't readily available. "A lemonade, perhaps? I'm sure there must be plenty of lemons in the kitchen. Henry?"

"No, thank you, Mrs. Wingate. Iced tea will be fine," Mike lied. What she'd really like was a beer. Or a double margarita. Two of them. Yes, two of them might just get her through the rest of the afternoon.

"Devlin, what would you like, dear?"

"I'll have a beer, thanks," he said to Henry, reaching across the table to pick up one of the dainty sandwiches. He glanced over at his mother before he bit into it. "Did *mémé* say if she'd be here tonight?"

"No, she didn't. She just said to expect her when we see her. You know as well as I do that that could be anytime between now and judgment day." Cecilia Wingate's smooth forehead was marred by a frown. "And this party was all her idea. *She* was the one who wanted to meet your new—" her cold blue eyes darted to Mike "—friend," she said, obviously unable to bring herself to utter the word fiancée in regard to Mike. She sighed again. "You'd think she'd have the good manners to be here."

"Well, I wouldn't worry about it," Devlin soothed. "She's sure to show up before the party's over."

Suddenly Trisha leaned forward in her chair. "Now I know where I've seen you before," she said, looking intently at Mike. "You're the chauffeur who brought Dev to the Dallas condo a week or so ago, aren't you?"

Unconsciously Mike lifted her chin. "Yes, I am." *Want to make something of it?*

"You're a *chauffeur*, Miss Frazer?" Cecilia Wingate's tone was scandalized.

"Not just a chauffeur." It was Devlin who responded to his mother's question. His glance toward Mike was proud and possessive. "Mike owns the Unicorn Limousine Service."

"But a . . . a chauffeur?" Cecilia Wingate repeated, as shocked as if Henry had had the audacity to sit down at the table with them.

Lunch went downhill from there.

THE PARTY WOULD PROBABLY be more of the same, Mike thought despairingly as she stood before the mirrored doors of the armoire and tugged at the bodice of the dress that Vicki had talked her into buying. What had seemed perfect in the confines of a department store dressing room looked woefully inadequate now.

The dress was made of gold-shot bronze silk and was—or so Vicki had said—the perfect color to complement her hair and skin tones. Exquisitely simple in design, it was cut on the bias to artfully outline each subtle curve of her body. Spaghetti straps bared her freckled arms and shoulders, a V-neck exposed the gentle swell of her breasts, and the narrow hem ended just below her knees.

Mike felt as exposed as if she were wearing a slip.

And she was absolutely sure that Cecilia Wingate would think it was highly improper and terribly lower-class. Just the sort of a dress a *chauffeur* would wear.

Well, there was nothing she could do about it now, Mike told herself sternly. She didn't have anything else

remotely suitable to wear to the party that was about
to begin downstairs. This was the only dress she had
brought with her and, besides, she liked it. At least, she
had liked it when she'd tried it on in the dressing room.

A week of basking in Devlin's undisguised admiration and desire had given her the confidence to believe
that she could wear a dress like this; that she could look
sexy and chic in it. Unfortunately, an afternoon with
his elegant and disapproving family was all it had taken
to disabuse her of that notion.

Mike sighed. Maybe she should just not go downstairs.

She thought about that for a moment, giving serious
consideration to staying in her room. Surely no one
would miss her. She sighed again. No, that wouldn't
work. The party was ostensibly being given to introduce her to Devlin's family. Someone was bound to
notice if she didn't show up. Still ... what if she sent
word down that she wasn't feeling well? She was sure
that the Wingates were far too well-bred to call her on
a little white lie. It would be an easy way out. The
coward's way out.

She scowled at her reflection. "Are you going to let
these snobby Wingates buffalo you?" she demanded of
the woman in the mirror. "They're just people. Plain
ordinary people. Nothing to be scared of. And you look
fine." Nervously she touched her moussed and blow-
dried hair, turning her head from side to side to make
sure the little gold button earrings were still fastened to
her ears. "Just fine," she repeated, smoothing a hand
down the front of her dress.

If only she didn't feel so damn naked!

Oh, well, Devlin will love it. She comforted herself with that thought, forgetting that she was still mad at him. At the moment he was her only friend in a house full of decidedly *un*friendly strangers. The only person she knew. She could murder him later.

"Devlin will love it," she whispered to herself as she crossed the thick cream carpet. "Devlin will love it. Devlin will love it." Taking a deep breath, she jerked open the bedroom door and stepped into the upstairs hall.

The sound of instruments being tuned drifted up the stairs. Violins, Mike thought, her head cocked as she listened. Violins and a piano. This was not going to be a small family party, she realized. People didn't hire musicians for small family parties. Not even people like the Wingates.

Damn Devlin for getting her into this! Murder was too good for him. She decided to torture him first. Slowly and with great pleasure. First, she'd string him up by those elegant thumbs of his, then she'd—

A low wolf whistle sounded behind her.

Mike whirled around, ready and eager to tell Devlin just what she thought of his low-down, sneaky, underhanded behavior. The angry words died in her throat.

He was gorgeous. Absolutely gorgeous. The traditional black tuxedo fit him to perfection, heightening his inherent elegance, accenting his masculinity. His shirt was snowy white against his golden skin, the front a masterpiece of fine knife pleats, the collar a dashing wing-tip. His bow tie was black satin to match his lapels and, instead of a cummerbund, he wore a low-cut snug-fitting black satin vest. His shirt studs and cuff links were onyx and gold.

Ohmigod.

"You look beautiful, sweetheart," he said warmly, his eyes raking over her as he took her hands in both of his. "Absolutely beautiful." He lowered his head, lifting her left hand to his mouth in a gesture as graceful as the man himself.

Mike tried desperately not to be affected by it. "I'm mad at you," she informed him frostily.

"Still?" He glanced up at her through his lashes as he lifted the other hand to his lips.

Stubbornly she ignored the look. "Yes, *still*," she said, giving him a narrow-eyed glare.

He turned her hand over and pressed his lips to her palm. "Why?"

"Why?" Her voice rose indignantly, but she didn't try to pull her hands away. "You dare to ask me *why*?"

He kissed the other palm. "Umm-hmm. Why?"

"Because you . . ." She faltered a bit when his lips touched the inside of her wrist. Bravely she gulped and went on. He wasn't using that sexy charm of his to get out of it this time. "Because you embarrassed me in front of your family, that's why. Because you said you wouldn't bring up this silly marriage thing and—"

"I don't think it's silly, Mike. I love you." He lowered their clasped hands, and his expression, as he stared down into her eyes, was deadly serious. "And you love me, too."

Slowly Mike shook her head. "No, I don't," she insisted. "I'm just infatuated with you. And...and you're just infatuated with me." Misery flooded through her as she uttered the words. "It won't last."

His smile was full of love. "Is that what you still think this is? Infatuation?"

"Yes."

"You're wrong, Michaelann." Their hands were still clasped, and he took a step closer. So close that their bodies touched lightly, whispers of heat connecting them at knee and hip and breast. Mike had to tilt her head back to look up at him. "I love you. No—" He stopped her when she would have denied it. "Just listen to me for a minute. I love you," he repeated softly. "And you love me. You might not recognize the emotion yet because it hasn't happened to you before, or because you don't have anything to compare it to. But I do. And I'm telling you, sweetheart, this is love. For both of us."

"We don't have anything in common." Her voice was halting, uncertain, unconsciously sad.

His hands tightened on hers for a moment. "We have *everything* in common."

"Name one thing," Mike challenged.

"You have thousands of freckles. And I—" he dropped a quick kiss on the tip of her nose "—love freckles."

"That's not what I meant."

"No? Well, then... We're both hardworking business people." He smiled slightly, knowing that Mike still wasn't quite convinced of that. "We're both native Texans." That was irrefutable. "We both like cold beer, and sour cream on our baked potatoes, and sautéed mushrooms with our steaks. We dance the two-step together as if we'd been born doing it."

"Hundreds of people could say the same thing, Devlin. That doesn't make them partners for life."

"It does if they love each other."

Mike shook her head. "We don't come from the same kind of people or have the same background. You're like...like fancy Russian caviar, and I'm just black-eyed peas."

"I love black-eyed peas." He grinned. "And I can't stand caviar."

"Devlin, I'm serious."

"So am I."

"Oh, Devlin." She closed her eyes for a moment, garnering the strength to resist him. It *was* only infatuation. And they *would* get over it. She could hear chamber music, all in tune now, drifting up the stairs, mingled with the sound of voices and soft laughter. It seemed to underscore the differences between them. A trembling sigh escaped her. "I'm not the kind of woman you should marry. Your mother—"

Devlin made a quick dismissive gesture. "My mother is a hopeless snob."

"But—"

"But nothing. I love you. You love me. We're getting married." He dropped a quick hard kiss on her parted lips and stepped back. "And that's final."

"Final, huh?" She heard the front door open again, letting in another group of his mother's guests. "We'll see about that." She slipped her hands out of his and turned toward the stairs, suddenly eager to run Cecilia Wingate's gantlet and have it over with. Maybe a dose of her social ineptness would convince Devlin that she was right.

His hand on her arm stopped her. "Wait a minute."

She paused, looking back over her shoulder.

"I have something for you." He put his free hand in his jacket pocket and pulled out something gold and glittering. "I wanted you to have it before we went downstairs."

"Devlin, not another present!" she objected, both scandalized and pleased at his extravagant generosity. It made her feel a bit guilty to accept his offerings while insisting that she wasn't going to marry him. "You've got to stop giving me presents all the time."

"Why? I like to give you presents. Here, turn around. No, this way, so I can fasten it." A long delicate gold chain dropped too quickly in front of her eyes for her to see what was dangling on it. Something small and heavy and cool bumped lightly against her chest. She touched it, trying to figure out what it was, as Devlin's fingers worked at the back of her neck. "There. It's fastened. Let me see." He turned her around to face him. "Beautiful. Just like you."

Mike lifted the pendant so she could see it. "A strawberry!" It was tiny and golden, perfectly detailed right down to the cap of leaves at the top and the seeds embedded in its flesh. "Oh, Devlin, it's beautiful. I—" A blush touched her cheeks as she remembered the last time he'd told her she tasted like strawberries. Petit fours and champagne came to mind. "How could you?"

That wicked, teasing grin broke over his face. "I just walked into the jewelry store and told 'em I wanted something specially made for a woman who tasted like strawberries."

"Devlin, you didn't!"

"Yes, I did." He plucked the tiny golden fruit from between her fingers and, holding it away from her body, leaned down and kissed the spot where it would rest. The warmth of his mouth seemed to radiate in all directions, like a sunburst exploding on her skin. Then he laid the pendant back in place, covering his kiss. "I want you to think of me each time you wear it."

"I will." Deeply moved, she reached up and touched his cheek. She knew without being told that he had given this to her now as a shield against her insecurities and fears in the midst of his family. "Thank you, Devlin."

He covered her hand with his, pressing it to his cheek for a moment before he brought it to his lips. "You're welcome, sweetheart."

Then, their fingers entwined, they headed down the stairs.

14

THE FIRST FIFTEEN MINUTES weren't too bad. Devlin was right by her side, touching her elbow or the small of her back as he introduced her to his friends and acquaintances. Mike was even beginning to think that she might have been wrong about a few other things, too. Her dress was fine: no less elegant, nor more indecent than any other woman's. If it lacked froufrou and flourishes, well, it was about time she admitted that she was not a froufrou type of woman.

She was fitting in okay, too. Not great, but okay. She could talk to Devlin's business associates with ease, commenting on the current economic climate with the insight of a savvy businesswoman. Interest rates and megatrends were things she knew about. Talking to the businessmen's wives was less easy, but she was doing that, too.

But then Mrs. Wingate advanced on them, declaring that Mike simply had to meet some of Pam and Trisha's friends, and things started to go downhill again.

Having introduced her to the group of chattering women, Cecilia Wingate left her there. Pam and Trisha's friends were cut from the same mold as Pam and Trisha themselves. While most of them were not as beautiful as Devlin's ebony-haired sisters, they were as polished and sleek and "in" as the two girls. They didn't mean to make Mike feel left out and inadequate—at least, she didn't think they did—but she felt that way just the same. They didn't seem to know what to say to her any more than she knew what to say to them.

"Pam tells me you're a chauffeur, Miss Frazer," one of them commented, finally turning to include the newcomer in the conversation. She was about twenty-three or so, a small fragile blonde in powder blue. A deep ruffle ran diagonally across her bodice, defining the neckline of her one-shouldered dress. Mike immediately began to feel gawky and awkward. "That must be very interesting work."

Mike fingered her strawberry pendant, glancing over to where Devlin was deep in conversation with his father and another man. "Actually, I own Unicorn Limousines," she said, realizing that she had been left to her own devices for the time being and would have to somehow manage. "I hardly drive anymore."

"*Oh*, you own your own business." The information obviously raised her a notch in the little blonde's estimation. "How interesting. Pam and I have a business, too. Don't we, Pam?" She appealed to the older of Devlin's sisters for confirmation. Pam nodded, but kept up her conversation with another woman. "We run a little art gallery in the Galleria. Not terribly big but quite select and exclusive. Daddy and Mr. Wingate loaned us the money to get started, and we found a simply excellent woman to take care of all the little day-to-day things. Bookkeeping is such a bore, don't you agree, Miss Frazer?"

"I, uh, do all my own bookkeeping," Mike admitted, wondering why she felt as if she were admitting to participating in weird sexual practices. "Although," she hastened to add, "I don't enjoy it nearly as much as getting out in the garage and tinkering under the hood."

"'Tinkering under the hood?' Oh, you mean you work on the cars? Like a mechanic? How interesting."

That word again, thought Mike. *Interesting.*

"Well, Pam and I work quite hard at our little shop, too," she said, obviously making an effort to find something to talk about. "In fact, we're off to Europe this fall to pick up more stock. Don't you just love Europe in the fall? Especially Italy. It's my absolute favorite. The shopping there is fabulous." She took a sip of her drink, something as frothy as she was. "What's your favorite country, Miss Frazer?"

"I don't know. I've never been to Europe."

"Well, you haven't missed all that much," she said kindly. "The good old U.S. of A. has plenty of culture and art if you know where to look. We get a great deal of our stock in New York. In fact, Pam discovered Tellman on her last trip there. He's very exciting, don't you think?"

Mike merely nodded, having no idea what, or who, Tellman was.

"My family has an apartment on 71st between Fifth and Madison, so it's very convenient for us to just run on up there whenever we need to. And, of course, it gives us the chance to absorb the culture and do some shopping. I have the hardest time staying out of the Trump Tower. I think all those beautiful shops are just too tempting, don't you?"

"I don't know. I've never been to New York. In fact," she said, unconsciously imitating the blonde's breathless way of talking, "I've never even been out of the state of Texas."

"Oh, I see . . ." The little blonde drifted off, having made as many conversational sallies as she was going to.

Mike stood there for another five minutes, stiff as a stick, and feeling uncomfortable as she wondered how to gracefully leave the fringes of the group. Did one just walk away? Or should she interrupt the conversation and excuse herself?

However it was to be done, she wanted to find Devlin or, failing that, she wanted to sneak up to her room and pack. Maybe they could leave first thing in the morning instead of staying on through what was sure to be another difficult luncheon with his family.

"Miss Frazer."

Thankful to be rescued, Mike turned toward Devlin's youngest sister, instinctively realizing that Trisha might be her only female ally at this party. "Please, call me Mike."

"Mike, then," Trisha amended with a smile. "A few of us are getting together for a few rounds of golf tomorrow after church. Would you like to join us?"

"I'm afraid I don't play golf," she admitted, her fingers fiddling with the tiny golden strawberry around her neck.

"Well, tennis, then," Trisha offered. "The club has excellent facilities. Six courts, so we can all play at the same time."

"I'm sorry, but I don't play tennis, either."

"Oh, well . . ." Mike could see her casting around in her mind for some other topic of conversation.

"Do you play bridge, Miss Frazer?" someone else asked.

Mike started looking around for a hole to crawl into. "No, I don't," she said apologetically, feeling as inadequate as she had when she was a teenager. Then her chin lifted, just as it always had then. *I will not let them intimidate me.* "I play a mean hand of stud poker, though."

"Stud poker?"

"Yes, my brothers taught me when we were kids. We used to play in the barn using penny nails for money." Some imp of mischief—or foolish bravado—seized her, making her bold. If they wanted a hick, well, dammit, she'd give them a hick. "Now, of course, I play in a regular Wednesday night game with the mechanics in my garage. For money." She grinned challengingly. "Any of you ladies care to make up a game tomorrow?"

A circle of startled faces met her question.

"No? Well, I think I'll just mosey on over to the bar and get me a beer, then. See if any of those gentlemen would like to play. Excuse me, ladies."

She made her way to the bar in record time and, seeing all the ingredients laid out, ordered a margarita instead of a beer. Lifting the frosty salt-rimmed glass to her lips, she glanced around the room, searching for Devlin—or, failing that, a way out.

She spotted him over by the wide double doors that led into the library, surrounded by a group of laughing people. A brunette with fuchsia sequins scattered over her size 38D bosom appeared to be hanging on his every word, smiling up at him as if he had just told the world's funniest joke.

Mike tipped her drink to her lips, recklessly downing half the contents in one long swallow. All she got for her trouble was an intense stab of pain between her eyes from the cold of the crushed ice. She pressed two fingers to the middle of her forehead until it passed, then sipped more slowly, all the while wondering if it would be too impolite to shove her way across the room to Devlin's side. She desperately needed a little reassurance.

Just then he looked up, scanning the room as if he were looking for someone. His eyes went past her for just a second, then backtracked as he caught the flash of her ginger hair. He smiled, silently beckoning her to join him.

Mike brightened instantly and began weaving her way cautiously through the crowd around the bar. Her progress was slow, and at one point she came to a complete standstill while she waited for two men whose backs were toward her to realize that she was behind them and wanted to get by.

"The contract turned out all right," the bigger man was saying.

Mike recognized the voice; he had been introduced to her earlier as one of Devlin's senior executives. He struck her as a quintessential good ol' boy, Texas right down to his hand-stitched cowboy boots. She lifted her hand to tap his shoulder and ask him to let her by, but the rest of his statement stopped her cold.

"I don't mind tellin' you, when Devlin first asked Parker Consulting to sign with that little lady's limousine service I thought sure he was just tossing some business to his latest little playtoy. Don't know that he still isn't doing just that, but I don't think it'll make no nevermind. Parker says she runs a sound company. Still, you know ol' Dev . . ." His booming voice had a jovial leer in it. "Generous to a fault with his women. Can't say as I blame him with this one, though. She's a looker all right, in spite of all them freckles."

The other man laughed, agreeing with his companion, and Mike turned on her heel, frantic to get away before they realized that she had been standing right behind them. Using her elbow to good advantage, she plowed through the crowd around the bar.

Throwing a little business to his latest little playtoy, was he! How dare he interfere with her business! How dare he make her the object of salacious gossip! She'd show him a playtoy all right!

Furious, she hurried out of the living room, across the hall and up the wide staircase to the second floor, taking the steps two at a time in her haste. She slammed the door of the cream-and-blue bedroom behind her, not caring in the least that the sound reverberated through the upper hall. Hauling her single suitcase out of the closet, she tossed it on the pale blue bedspread and began throwing her few clothes into it.

How dare he, she thought again, hot tears stinging her eyes as she remembered how he'd shown up at her office with champagne and petit fours to celebrate her business triumph. *Her business triumph!* That was a joke.

She'd thought she'd gotten the account on her own because Unicorn Limousines had a reputation as a dependable company, because she'd put on such a good presentation, because she was such a great businesswoman. Ha! If she'd walked into Parker Consulting with spiked hair and motorcycle leathers and the contract printed in red crayon, she'd still have gotten it signed on the dotted line.

Ol' Dev's latest little playtoy.

Damn him!

She snapped the suitcase shut, dragged it off the bed and stormed out of the bedroom, slamming the door again for good measure. She ran into Devlin halfway down the stairs.

"Mike, what's the matter? Where are you going?"

She ignored him, staring straight ahead as she hurried down the stairs.

"Mike, answer me. What's the matter? What happened?" He thought at first that she was hurt, that someone had said something to wound her feelings. *Dammit,* he found himself thinking, *if Mother's said anything to hurt her, I'll . . .* He put his hand over hers on the handle of the suitcase, halting her on the bottom step. "Mike, stand still and tell me what's the matter."

"Let go of my suitcase."

"Sweetheart, wait a minute." He reached out with his free hand, turning her face to his. "Just tell me what's the matter."

She looked at him with eyes of gold-shot emerald simmering with a furious, roiling anger. And it was directed at him. Not at someone who might have hurt her feelings. At him. He couldn't begin to imagine what he had done to make her look like that.

"Don't call me sweetheart," she said through clenched teeth. "And let go of my suitcase." She jerked away, heading for the door. A path cleared for her as she crossed the wide hall and fascinated spectators fell back to give her way. Henry opened the door before she reached it and kept holding it as Devlin rushed out after her.

"Just what in hell do you think you're doing?" he demanded, grabbing her arm as she reached for the car door.

"I'm leaving. What does it look like?"

"Why?"

"Because it's a lousy party, that's why. Now let go of me."

"Mike, I'm warning you . . ."

"Warning me! You're warning me? Of all the—" Mike shook his hand off and yanked open the door of the MG. "Well, this is one little *playtoy* who isn't listening to any of your warnings." She tossed her suitcase behind the seat and slid behind the wheel.

"Playtoy? What the hell are you talking about?"

Mike leveled a look at him. "Parker Consulting," she said succinctly, daring him to deny it.

But Devlin didn't deny it. He knew he was caught. "Who told you?"

"Does it matter? I know, that's enough."

"Yes, dammit, it matters—"

She yanked at the door handle, trying to close it, but Devlin wouldn't let her. "Now wait just one minute, Mike. We have to talk about this."

"Write me a letter." She yanked again, and the door slammed shut, barely missing Devlin's fingers in the process. She jammed the key into the ignition.

Realizing that nothing he could say was going to stop her, Devlin raced around the front of the car and vaulted into the passenger seat.

"Get out of my car," she said coldly, not even bothering to look at him as she calmly fastened her seat belt.

"No, dammit. You came with me. If you want to leave, you're leaving with me." He crossed his arms over his chest. "So drive the damn thing!"

Tight-lipped, Mike gunned the engine to life. Not sparing a thought for her precious MG, she stomped on the gas pedal, releasing the clutch with her other foot, and shot around the fountain in the middle of the circular driveway.

She didn't see the taxi that had just turned in until it was almost too late to avoid a collision. Her teeth clenched against a startled scream, she swung the wheel hard to the right, missing the taxi by inches, and plowed through a narrow border of flowers, smack into the tinkling fountain. The impact snapped her head forward, then back, tossing her against the door with enough force to bruise her shoulder. The fountain cracked, wobbled on its pedestal for a moment, then crashed down on the hood of the MG. Water sprayed upward, wetting everything—the fine leather upholstery, Mike, her suitcase—on the way down. Mike didn't even notice.

Devlin sat slumped in the passenger seat, silent and unmoving. The shattered windshield bore mute testimony to how he had gotten that way.

Panic clutched her heart, driving everything else out. "Devlin! Devlin, are you all right?" Fumbling, her fingers numb with shock, Mike wrestled with the clip on her seat belt. "Oh, God, please," she prayed. It came loose finally, and she flung it aside, scrambling across the gear shift to gather his limp body into her arms. Gently she lifted his head, smoothing back the wet hair to see what damage she had caused. Her hand came away sticky with blood. "Oh, Devlin! My God, Devlin!" She looked up, frantic, calling to the people who were rushing down the steps to their aid. "Call a doctor, somebody, please. He's bleeding. Call a doctor." She looked back at the unconscious man, her eyes wild. "Oh, Devlin, I'm sorry. Please don't be hurt." Somebody put his hands under her arms and gently dragged her out of the car and away from Devlin so that they could tend to him but she seemed unaware of it. "Please don't be hurt, Devlin. I'm sorry. I'm sorry."

"I think this little gal needs something to calm her down," a voice said close to her ear. She thought it was a woman, but she couldn't be sure. "She's a mite hysterical."

"I'm all right," Mike insisted. "I'm all right. Ask them to look at Devlin. Please." Her voice was thin and reedy, like a frightened child's. Her eyes were huge and unseeing. "Devlin's bleeding."

"He's goin' be jes fine, missy. Don't you fret yourself none. He's comin' around already. See there? He's sittin' up and actin' sassy."

Mike looked where the woman pointed, but she couldn't see anything except a tight knot of people surrounding her car. It was raining. How could it be raining, she thought, when it was so hot out?

"You, Trisha," the voice demanded, "help me get her up these stairs." It fell to a soothing murmur again. "We'll jes get you put to bed, little gal. Don't you worry, Devlin'll be fine."

They got her into the house and up the stairs to the bedroom. Someone undressed her and tucked her into bed, keeping her there until the doctor could come and check her over. She was a bit bruised, he said, and slightly hysterical, but nothing that a good night's sleep wouldn't cure. She felt something cold prick her arm, and then nothing. Blackness closed over her.

15

FOR A MINUTE Mike didn't know where she was. The room was shadowed, the only light coming from a silk-shaded lamp on the bedside table. She was warm and kind of woozy in her mind, and—she shifted around a bit under the covers to verify it—she was naked. That surprised her because she never slept in the raw. Someone must have put her to bed.

Mike turned her head on the pillow and met Devlin's eyes staring at her out of the wrinkled face of the tiny woman who was sitting by her bed. She wore a robe made of some fuzzy greeny-blue material with embroidery on the collar and cuffs. The white ruffle of a nightgown showed at the neck. Her hair was black, and it hung in a fat braid over her left shoulder. There was a ball of pale yarn in her lap and knitting needles, still now, in her gnarled hands. She was, as Mike's father would have said, no bigger than a minute.

"So you're the little gal who's got my grandson so worked up," she said matter-of-factly, her eyes considering as she studied Mike. The knitting needles began to move again. "Well, you sure aren't the kind I thought he'd pick," she added bluntly. Her expression turned suddenly gleeful. "Does my poor heart good to know I was wrong."

Mike just stared at the woman. Without a doubt, this was Devlin's adored *Mémé* Lucie. She wasn't at all what Mike had expected, being tiny and wrinkled and unmistakably "country" instead of the haughty French aristocrat of Mike's imaginings. But she was definitely Devlin's grandmother. There was no mistaking the resemblance.

"I was scairt to death he was goin' to get himself one of those good-for-nothin' snub-nose deb-u-tantes." She said the word in three distinct syllables, as if it were three separate words. "Should'a knowed he had more sense than that. He's just like his granddaddy. Got a mind of his own, thanks be to God." She gave a satisfied little nod, and Mike recognized Devlin in the gesture. "And knows how to use it, too."

"Is he all right?"

"Who, Devlin? Shoot!" She cackled softly. "It'd take more 'n a whack on the head to keep him down. Don't fret yourself none, missy, he's jes fine, exceptin' for a little cut above his eye." She leaned forward in her chair and peered at Mike. "How're you doin'?"

"Okay, I guess." She moved gingerly under the covers, testing for aches and pains. "My left arm feels like somebody worked me over with a baseball bat. And I'm a little woozy." She made a tasting gesture with her tongue. "My mouth feels like it's full of cotton."

"That'll be the shot the doc gave you." *Mémé* stood up, reaching for the glass on the bedside table, and lifted it to Mike's lips. "Have a good long sip o' this."

Mike drank half the water in the glass. "Thank you," she said, lying back down on the pillows.

"You're right welcome, missy." She sat back down in the chair and picked up her knitting. The needles clacked rhythmically against each other. "Now, you mind tellin' me what got you so distracted that you ran that pretty little car of yours into Cissy's fountain to keep from hittin' my taxi?"

"Devlin and I were having a . . . a discussion."

"You were fightin', you mean?"

Mike nodded.

"Then say what you mean, gal. I don't hold with no pussyfootin' around."

"Devlin and I were fighting," Mike said obediently. "And I . . . I got so mad that I just stomped on the gas pedal without looking where I was going. But, dammit, he's so arrogant and—" She stopped, hesitant to criticize Devlin in front of his grandmother. Any fool could see that she was as crazy about him as he was about her.

"Spit it out, gal. You'll feel a whole heap better when you do."

"He can't take no for an answer, not about anything." Mike sat up in the bed, holding the blankets to her chest with one hand as she plumped the pillows behind her with quick jabs of her fist. Settling against them so that she was comfortable, she continued. "And he went right ahead and stuck his nose in my business, even after I told him I didn't want his help! And, well—" She shrugged. "I found out about it at the party and decided to leave. Devlin insisted he was coming with me."

Mémé nodded knowingly. "His granddaddy was that way. Used to make me so dern mad, tellin' me things I already knew more about 'n he did, I near parted his hair with my skinnin' knife. More'n once, too. But that's what gives a marriage spice, gal. Don't let it fret you none."

"But I'm not marrying Devlin."

Mémé didn't drop a stitch. "That isn't what I heard," she said tartly.

"From who? Devlin?"

"Who else would I be hearin' it from?"

"Who else, indeed?"

"He asked you, didn't he, gal?"

"Oh, yes. He asked me all right." She tucked the blankets more securely under her arms. "And I said no. Several times."

"Humph. I don't hold much with leadin' a man on. Tends to make 'em a mite unreasonable. But that's your business, gal. Jes don't be too long about it, you hear?" She shot Mike a piercing look. "I want to bounce my grandson's younguns on my knee before I die."

"You mean you don't mind that Devlin wants to marry me?"

"Mind? Why, land sake's, gal, 'course I don't mind. Where'd you get a fool notion like that? No, don't tell me," she said when Mike opened her mouth to answer. "Cissy and them two girls of hers, I'll be bound. Don't you pay them no mind, you hear? Why, you're just the sort of little gal I always hoped my boy'd marry."

Mike shook her head. "I wouldn't work, *mémé*," she said, not even realizing that she'd used Devlin's pet name for his grandmother. "We're just too different."

"'Course you're different. He's a man, and you're a woman, aren't you? You're supposed to be different."

"*Mémé*." Mike pinned her with a level look. "That's not what I meant, and you know it."

Lucie Bouvier Wingate met Mike's look with one of her own. "I know what you meant, gal. Don't think I don't. But none of that's important; not so long as you love my boy. And you do love him, don't you?"

Mike was silent for a moment.

Did she love Devlin Wingate?

Not just the physical stuff, she told herself sternly, and aside from the fact that he epitomized her every fantasy—romantic or otherwise. Aside, too, from the fact that he was more fun to be with than anyone else she knew and that she missed him when he wasn't around. And not taking into consideration the way he made her feel—special and desirable and feminine. Discounting all that, did she love him?

Could she be in love with a man who was as arrogant as a lord? A man who couldn't take no for an answer and always wanted his own way? A man who could make her angrier with just a lift of his eyebrow than anyone else could by screaming obscenities at her? And she'd been angry—mad as fire—when she'd found out what he'd done at Parker Consulting. But she'd been hurt, too, she realized. Maybe even more hurt than angry, because his action meant that he didn't have enough confidence in her ability to get the contract on her own. And, yes, dammit, that hurt: she wanted Devlin to believe in her.

And when she thought he'd been badly hurt after she'd crashed the MG into the fountain...what did her reactions to that say about her feelings for him? She'd been in accidents before, and she'd dealt with emergencies on her father's farm and in her own garage before, but she had never thought she was going to die from fear. She would have done anything to take his hurt onto herself when she looked over and saw him slumped against the dashboard. Anything.

Was that love? The true, forever after, getting married kind of love that Devlin insisted it was?

"Yes," she said at last. "I love him."

"Well, that's all that matters, gal. The rest will work itself out. Jes give it time."

"How can you be so sure of that?"

"Lord a'mighty. Look at me, missy. Do I look like a dyed-in-the-wool Wingate lady to you? 'Course not," she answered her own question before Mike could open her mouth. "I haven't ever been, and I don't ever want to be, neither. A more useless gaggle of hens ..." She snorted in disgust and leaned forward, letting her knitting fall idle in her lap. "Let me tell you somethin', missy. I was seventeen when I first met Devlin's granddaddy. He'd hired my pa to take him huntin' in the bayou, and I went along, too, 'course, because the dogs were mine. Well, damned if the only huntin' my Jonathan done was of me. Pert' near chased me all over the swamps," she declared, chuckling at the memory. "Let him catch me, too, after I decided he wasn't jes of a mind to trifle with me. We were married in a little crossroads church less'n a week later, and he brought me back here to this very house, just like a huntin' trophy that he meant to hang on the wall. And I tell you, little gal—" her eyes, so much like Devlin's, bored into Mike's "—I was plum scairt out of my shoes."

"What happened?"

"Oh, me and his ma started right off to buttin' heads, 'course. There wasn't anything she could do to get us unmarried, so she was bound and determined to make me into a true Wingate lady." *Mémé* chuckled again and sat back. The knitting needles started clacking again. "And I was bound and determined to stay jes the way my Jonathan found me. We settled it after a while, 'course, with both of us givin' and takin' a bit."

"Were you happy with him?"

"Happy? Why land sake's, gal. Would I have stayed around if I wasn't? 'Course I was happy!" She chuckled reminiscently. "That's not to say we didn't have our share of fightin'. My Jonathan could be as contrary as the devil himself and never did like to hear no for an answer."

Mike giggled. "He sounds just like Devlin."

"That he was." She smiled mistily, lost in her memories for a moment, and Mike had a glimpse of the seventeen-year-old girl she must have been. "Devlin has the look of my Jonathan around his mouth, and the same way of tiltin' his head when he's set to tease about somethin'. It takes me back jes to look at him sometimes." She sighed. "I only wish my son could'a got some of that charm. It would'a done him a world of good."

"Devlin's father?"

Mémé nodded. "Robert's a true Wingate, through and through," she admitted sadly. "Takes himself a mite bit too serious to my way of thinkin'. And that wife of his! Cissy means well, but she was a deb-u-tante, you know." *Mémé* sniffed disdainfully. "One of those society hens, all puffed up with her own importance and worryin' all the time about what other people are thinkin'. Those two girls aren't much better, either. Pretty as the mornin', both of them, but not a thought between 'em what doesn't have to do with clothes and parties and who's doin' what to who at that fancy country club of theirs." She looked up from her knitting, pinning Mike to the bed with eyes the exact color of Devlin's. "Do you really want to abandon my poor boy to such a fate?"

"Well . . ." Mike hesitated. *Mémé's* example hadn't been lost on her, but still . . . everything had happened so fast. When it came right down to it, she'd known Devlin less than two full weeks, despite the fact that it felt as though she'd known him for years.

"I know he's as high-handed as they come," *Mémé* commiserated with her. "He wants his own way all the time, won't take no for an answer. That can be tryin' on a woman." She sighed, sending Mike a sly look from under her lashes. "But he can be as purely sweet as honeysuckle on the vine, and there isn't a mean bone in his whole body. And, like my Jonathan, when he loves, he loves true." She leaned over and patted Mike's hand where it lay on the bedspread. "You think on it, missy."

Mike thought on it—for about one minute. So she had known him less than two weeks. So what? She loved him. That was the important thing, wasn't it? "*Mémé*, do you think anybody would mind if I just sort of went down the hall to check on him?" she asked, wanting to know if someone was keeping a watch at his bedside as *Mémé* had been doing at hers. "I mean, if he's not too hurt to see me. I—"

"Land sake's, no, gal. I told you, he's jes fine. The doc took a couple of little ol' stitches in his head, is all. Nothin' serious." *Mémé* bustled up out of her chair, setting her knitting aside, and snatched Mike's robe off the foot of the bed. "You just snuggle right into this," she said, holding the kimono-style garment open so that Mike could slip her arms into it. "Trot right on down there now, you hear?" she ordered gleefully. "Put my poor boy out of his misery."

Mike nodded and moved silently across the plush cream carpet. She quietly opened the bedroom door and peeked out. All clear. "Wish me luck, *mémé*," she said and slipped out into the hall with Lucie Wingate's warm chuckle still ringing in her ears.

The soft golden glow of a silk-shaded lamp left burning on a graceful side table lit the way for her. Carefully she counted doorways. Devlin was three rooms down from her, at the end of the wide hall. She tapped lightly on the door, then, receiving no answer, dropped her hand to the doorknob. Turning it slowly, she pushed the door open.

This room, too, was bathed in shadows. The faint glow of a night-light cast a warm pool of light in the far corner. Moonlight poured in through the open drapes in the window, trailing across the carpet to fall over Devlin's bed. A soft summer breeze stirred the transparent sheers, billowing them inward with the scent of night-blooming flowers caught in the gauzy folds.

Devlin was sleeping peacefully. He was lying on his back with one arm curled above his head and the other flung wide as if to claim the whole bed for himself. A pale sheet, bleached to white in the moonlight, was drawn up to the level of his navel. His chest was bare, lifting and falling easily with the cadence of his breathing. There was a stark white bandage on the right side of his forehead.

Mike padded silently across the carpeted floor and looked down at him. Slowly she let her breath out. The bandage wasn't nearly as big as she'd feared it would need to be to stop the awful flow of blood that had poured from the wound underneath it. His color was good. Just as smooth and golden as always. *Mémé* hadn't lied to her: aside from the cut on his head, he was all right.

Mike lowered herself to the edge of the bed and gently, carefully, stroked his silky hair, lifting it up and away from the bandage. "Devlin?" she whispered.

He mumbled something unintelligible and moved his head into her hand with a little nestling gesture. Mike felt her heart turn over with love.

"Devlin?"

He made another snuffling noise and shifted on the bed, turning his body toward her.

"Devlin, wake up." She bent over and placed her lips next to his ear. The strawberry pendant around her neck trailed across his shoulder. "Wake up, darling," she murmured, the endearment slipping out without her even noticing it. "I have something to tell you." She kissed his ear. "Something important."

Devlin's eyes fluttered open, and his hands came up to clasp her by the shoulders. "I already know what it is," he said sleepily, but the smile on his face was a sight to behold.

Mike drew back slightly. "You do?"

"Uh-huh." He pulled her firmly against his chest and put one hand behind her head. "You love me," he said arrogantly, and kissed her.

It was a long sweet kiss, warm and tender and wonderful. Mike sighed into his mouth, and her hands moved caressingly over the curve of his bare shoulders, loving the feel of him beneath her fingers. Loving, too, the feel of his man's body hardening against her hip. It told her, for sure, that he really hadn't been badly hurt in the accident; he couldn't feel this good, be this warm and strong and passionate, if he were badly hurt.

Reassured, she pressed closer to his warmth. Devlin tightened his arms, murmuring love words against her mouth, and tried to roll her beneath him. The movement forced a groan from his lips.

"Devlin?" Mike sat up as far as his encircling arms would allow, her hands suddenly motionless on his shoulders. "Devlin, what is it? Are you all right?"

"I forgot," he said ruefully, dropping back against the pillows.

"Forgot?" She eased out of his embrace, afraid that any sudden move would hurt him again. "Forgot what, darling? What is it?"

"The doctor warned me that I'd probably wake up feeling like a train had run over me." He shot her a teasing look, grinning despite his aching muscles and the dull throb that had started in his head. "But then you came in here and started seducing me, and I forgot." His expression urged her to share his small joke.

But Mike wasn't looking at his face just then. "Where does it hurt?" she asked, her hands skimming lightly over his shoulders and chest, looking for hidden injuries. "Should I call someone? *Mémé*? Or your mother?"

"God, no!" He caught both her hands in one of his and pressed them against his chest. "I'm fine, Mike. I don't need anyone." He lifted her chin with his other hand, holding it still until she looked at him. "Except you, sweetheart."

Her insides turned to mush. "Oh, Devlin."

He pushed the sheet aside. "Come in with me."

She hesitated, torn by what she wanted to do and what she knew she should do. He'd been injured; he needed his rest. Mike shook her head. "We can't, Devlin. You're not well enough."

He gave her a look of injured innocence. "I just want to hold you."

"Oh... Well, I guess that's all right." She started to climb into the bed beside him.

"Take that robe off first."

"You said you just wanted to hold me."

"I do. I am. But I want to feel your skin against mine while I do it, okay?"

"Devlin," she said warningly, but she was already shrugging the robe off her shoulders.

"My God, you're all bruised, too!"

"Just my arm," she said, glancing down at the purple bruise that spread from just below her shoulder down to her elbow. "It looks worse than it is. Serves me right for driving like a maniac."

He touched the bruise with gentle fingertips. "It was my fault."

"No, it wasn't," she said firmly. "*I* was the one driving, and I should have known better than to let my feelings get behind the wheel with me."

"That was my fault, too." His expression was pained and almost sheepish.

"What was your fault, too?"

"You were driving like a maniac because you were angry at me over Parker Consulting."

There was a moment of silence. She hadn't intended to bring this up now, but since he had, they might as well get a few things clear from the start. She loved him, yes. And she was going to marry him, too, if he still wanted her. But she wasn't going to have him interfering in her business, doing things behind her back, even if he did think it was for her own good. Unicorn Limousines was *her* business, and she would run it just the way she always had. He might as well know it now instead of later.

Mike sighed. "Yes, I was mad at you, Devlin. The thought that you'd do something like that— That you'd make me look like some birdwitted idiot in front of a client made me furious. But it hurt me, too," she said slowly, trying to put her feelings into words. "To think that you thought that I needed that kind of help. That you didn't believe I could get the account on my own. I could've, you know." She pinned him with a look. "I've been running Unicorn Limousines quite successfully for some time now."

"I know. I know. I was wrong to interfere in your business without talking it over with you first," he said, surprising her with his candor. "I knew it even while I was doing it, but I didn't think you'd let me help you if you knew about it."

"You're right. I wouldn't."

"If it's any consolation, I didn't actually order Parker to make the deal. I just sort of suggested that he might want to give it his personal attention."

She sent him a dry censuring look, knowing just how such a "suggestion," coming from the president of the company, would sound to an employee. He wasn't fooling her one bit—and he knew it.

"Besides, I didn't think you'd ever find out about it."

"Devlin!"

"I know. I know." He put the back of his hand against his forehead as if overcome by shame. "It was a rotten thing to do—trying to make things a little easier for the woman I love." The eyes behind his concealing hand were alight with a teasing glow. "I don't know what came over me. It was underhanded, sn—"

"Devlin," she said warningly, trying hard not to laugh. She was not going to let him get away with this— or let him think that he could do it again whenever he felt like it. Her business was important to her. The most important thing in her life until two weeks ago. "Devlin, this isn't a laughing matter," she said sternly.

He lowered his hand. "I know. I'm sorry." He trailed a finger down her arm, then gazed up at her. "Forgive me?"

As simply as that, it was over and done with. "Yes, of course, I forgive you, Devlin." She lifted the sheet and swung her legs onto the bed. "Just don't do it again. Now move over." She lay down beside him, careful not to snuggle too close to his abused body.

Devlin curled an arm around her shoulders. "Closer."

"But your side."

"My side is no worse than yours, Mike. And if you can stand it, I can."

"But—"

"But nothing." He pulled her closer and pressed her head to his shoulder, effectively silencing her half-hearted protests. "I need to feel you next to me."

With a soft sigh Mike nestled into the crook of his arm as if she had been doing it all her life. She laid her hand on the wide expanse of his bare chest, actually liking the way its pale freckled surface looked against the darkness of his skin. "Is this okay? Are you comfortable?"

"Perfect." He lifted her hand from his chest, kissed the palm, and then laid it back down, covering it with his own.

Mike sighed again, for pure happiness, and rubbed her cheek against his shoulder, as much at ease as a kitten in familiar hands. Then, thinking of some unfinished business, she pushed herself up on one elbow, placed her hand on the hard curve of his pectoral muscle, and propped her chin on the back of it.

"How do you know I love you?" she demanded, gazing up into his face with adoring eyes. "I haven't actually said it yet."

Devlin grinned lazily, more at peace with himself at this moment than he had ever been in his life. "Say it now," he invited.

"I love you, Devlin." She pressed her lips to his chest and then looked up into his eyes. "But how did you know? For sure, I mean?"

He laughed softly. "Because you were more worried about me than that precious car of yours."

"My car? Oh, the MG." A sudden picture of it flashed through her mind: the mangled hood, crushed beneath the weight of the broken fountain; the spraying water that soaked the leather upholstery. The picture didn't bring the same sick feeling that it might have just a few days ago, and she realized he was right. Her first thought *had* been about Devlin...and her second...and her third. She hadn't thought about the car at all until just this minute. And she still didn't want to think about it; she was feeling too good to worry about mangled metal and repair bills.

And if that wasn't love, then nothing was.

"Your grandmother came to see me tonight," she murmured, slowly circling his nipple with the tip of her finger.

"I know." Devlin's voice and expression were smug. "I sent her."

Mike ignored his interruption. "She seems to think that you're in terrible danger of getting all puffed up with your own importance."

Devlin's hand drifted lazily down her back. "She does, huh?"

"Yes." Mike nodded seriously. "And I have her blessing to see that it doesn't happen. She's glad I'm not one of those 'good-for-nothin' snub-nose deb-u-tantes.'" She drawled the word disparagingly, the way *mémé* did. "She doesn't think a debutante would know how to keep you in line." She grinned at him. "Seems you're a lot like your rascally granddaddy."

Devlin grinned back at her. "Does this mean you're going to marry me?" The words were said lightly, as a joke, but the expression in his eyes was deadly serious.

"Yes." There was an awed sort of surprise in Mike's husky voice, and her eyes were huge and shining as she gazed back at him. "Why, yes, I guess it does."